MW00411763

Tales of the Were
Grizzly Cove

Mating
Dance

BIANCA D'ARC

This book is a work of fiction. The names, characters, places, and incidents are products of the writer's imagination or have been used fictitiously and are not to be construed as real. Any resemblance to persons, living or dead, actual events, locale or organizations is entirely coincidental.

No part of this book may be used or reproduced in any manner whatsoever without written permission, except in the case of brief quotations embodied in critical articles and reviews.

DEDICATION

With much love and many thanks to my family, without whom I would never have become a writer in the first place.

I'd also like to thank my fantastic editor, Jessica Bimberg. You're awesome to work with, Jess!

And last, but certainly not least, many thanks to the readers who continue to make this all possible. Your support throughout the years has been invaluable and I sincerely hope you enjoy our time together in Grizzly Cove...

CHAPTER ONE

Tom Masdan was the one and only lawyer in Grizzly Cove, Washington, and he liked it that way. Tom figured if there was more than one lawyer in a town, they'd be obligated to fight things out in court, which was one aspect of his profession that he loathed. The conflict of the adversarial process annoyed his inner bear and made him want to scratch, claw and just beat his opponent into submission rather than wait to hear what some old guy wearing a dress and sitting on a podium had to say.

Tom thought, not for the first time, that maybe studying law hadn't been the brightest idea he'd ever had. Then again, shifters needed legal representation every once in awhile, just like everybody else. That's where he came in.

He enjoyed helping people like himself—

people who lived under the radar of the human population. Shapeshifters had to learn to adapt to the modern, human world. That included following the laws of the countries in which they lived.

Tom had been born and raised in the United States. He'd gone to an Ivy League law school back east. Since then, he had offered his services solely to the *were* of North America, or any *were* that needed legal representation in the States. He filed claims, did a lot of paperwork, and helped shapeshifters of all kinds create the paper trail that humans found so necessary to their existence.

He had traveled all over, but he had never found the one woman who could complete him. He'd never found his mate.

So when his long-time friend, John Marshall—known simply as Big John to most folks—proposed the idea of forming their own little enclave on the Washington coast and putting out an open call for any bear shifters who wanted to move there, Tom was cautiously optimistic. The idea of gathering a relatively large group of usually solitary bears in one town was both novel and intriguing. It could also be dangerous as hell, but Tom trusted Big John's ultra-Alpha tendencies to keep everybody in line.

John had asked Tom to begin the process of turning the large, adjoining parcels of real estate John had bought over the past several years into a new town. There were lots of forms to file with the state of Washington, and quite a few building contracts to oversee. He'd also overseen the real estate deals of neighboring properties for each of the core group of bear shifters that had joined John on this quest. It had taken a good portion of the last several years of Tom's life, but the town of Grizzly Cove had finally become a reality.

It was a really good reality too. The town was small by human standards, but already a few dozen bear shifters had answered John's call for settlers. There were still more males than females, but with the recent decision to allow a few select human-owned businesses to open up on Main Street, things were beginning to change.

Just last week, the sheriff had found his mate in the human woman who, along with her two sisters, owned the new bake shop. It was a true mating, and Tom was happy for them.

But, it had become clear that the so-called secret of Grizzly Cove hadn't really been that much of the secret to the other two sisters. They'd taken the news about shapeshifters in stride. It seemed they'd already figured it out.

Which meant that the shifter residents weren't being careful enough. And that the two remaining sisters needed to agree not to spill the beans.

A job for Tom, the Alpha had said. Tom wasn't so sure. He might be a lawyer, but he wasn't necessarily a smooth talker. He did his best work on a computer, in an office. He wasn't the kind of attorney who schmoozed clients over three-martini lunches.

But Big John had asked him to try, so there Tom was, approaching the bakery he had never stepped foot in before. It wasn't that he was shy. It was more that he hadn't really wanted to interact with the new humans in town until the experiment had been proven a success. The bakery was the first of many applications Tom had received from business people who wanted to open stores in their town.

The decision had been made to allow the bakery—and the three sisters—as a trial run.

Their food was excellent, from all accounts, and most of the shifters in town liked the women and were glad one of their comrades had found a mate.

Humans made decent mates, and bears couldn't be picky. There weren't a lot of bears in the first place, and it wasn't uncommon for them to find mates outside their species. A lot of bear shifters took human mates. It didn't diminish the magic. Bears had more than most shifters, and Tom often thought, that's why they were kind of rare. But what did he know? Only the Mother of All—the Goddess who watched over all shifters—knew for certain.

The bell over the door tinkled as Tom pushed into the bakery. Immediately, he was surrounded by the most scrumptious scents of baking bread, honey and some kind of cheese. He took stock of the place and realized he was the only customer this early in the day. Only one of the sisters was there, working in the back.

That would be the middle sister, he'd been told. She worked the morning shift, and her name was Ashley Baker. The irony of the Baker sisters owning a bakery had struck Tom as suspicious when he'd first seen their application, but he'd done thorough background checks on all three women, and they really were named Baker and had been since their birth.

The blonde woman came out from behind one of the ovens, wiping her hands on her apron as she greeted him. She took up her position behind the counter with a brisk sort of efficiency, and Tom was struck momentarily dumb when she smiled.

"Good morning," she said brightly. "What can I get for you?"

Sonuva... Tom's bear sat up and wanted to roar. It liked the woman.

Hell, it more than *liked* her. It was thinking *mate*.

No way.

Tom cleared his throat, realizing the woman was looking at him strangely. She'd asked him something...

Oh, yeah. She wanted to know why he was there. He stuck his hand out over the counter with a jerky movement.

"Hi, I'm Tom. Tom Masdan."

Smooth, buddy. Real smooth. Tom grimaced inwardly at his own awkwardness.

She wiped her hand once more and took his for a brisk shake. She was eyeing him with a sort of amused wariness as she looked more closely at him.

"You're the town lawyer. I recognize your name from the contracts we signed when we moved in."

His turn to talk. Dammit. He wasn't ready for this. He'd been caught completely flat-footed by the woman. His discomfort turned to anger as he shook her hand. Anger at himself, for being such a dork.

Then he got lost in the feel of her soft skin against his palm. She was delicate and womanly, and her hand held a faint grit of powder. Probably flour, he reasoned with the small part of his brain that was still functioning.

She was looking at him strangely again. Oh, yeah. He was supposed to say something.

"Yeah, uh…" He cleared his throat as she withdrew her hand, and he had to let her go. He didn't want to let her go, but he couldn't very well drag her over the top of the counter by her fingertips, now, could he? "Yes. I'm the lawyer."

Also, apparently, he was an idiot. Stating the obvious. He mentally kicked himself and cleared his throat again, looking around the bakery, searching for something to say that wouldn't make him appear even stupider. Breathing in the delicious aromas, he was struck with inspiration.

"So, uh, what are you baking back there? It smells really good."

She smiled again. He'd said the right thing.

"I've got one oven full of artisanal breads, a tray of honey buns, and I'm just putting the finishing touches on some cheese danish. Any of that strike your fancy? The danish are delish." Was she teasing him or was this her normal manner? He couldn't be sure, having stayed far away from the Baker sisters since they'd moved in.

"I'll have a danish if they're ready," he replied, needing time to think.

He asked her for a cup of coffee too and decided to stay for a bit, using one of the tables scattered around the front of the shop to eat and spend time getting his sanity back.

She moved away from the counter as he scrambled for equilibrium. She bustled around in the back for a bit, but it wasn't long before she returned with a cheesy confection on a plate that smelled really good. Tom's stomach grumbled as she placed the steaming cup of coffee next to the plate on a small tray. He paid her for the snack and took his tray to the closest table without another word.

CHAPTER TWO

Ashley Baker was intrigued by the tall man. He'd seemed gruff and a little odd, but maybe he was just having a bad morning or something. It was early, even for the early risers of Grizzly Cove. The sun was just barely breaking over the mountain to the east, painting the dark waters of the cove in cheery golden ripples. It was her favorite time of day, and she seldom shared it with anyone, for the simple reason that nobody ever really came into the bakery this early.

Normally, she would take a break as dawn arrived, sipping her coffee while staring out at the waters of the cove, the sun rising from behind her, giving her a stunning view of the cove and the wildlife that inhabited it. She saw all kinds of birds, even a few seals occasionally. And she had a pet seagull she threw crumbs to every morning when he

10

came up to the door of the bakery.

Sure enough, there he was now. Ashley grabbed the little dish of bread crumbs she saved for the old bird and headed for the door.

"If you feed that thing, you'll have the whole flock here in no time," the man said as she approached the door.

Ashley laughed. "Gus and I have an understanding. You'll see."

"Gus?" Tom got to his feet.

He walked closer while Ashley opened the door of the bakery and stepped out. She wasn't surprised when Tom followed, though she noticed he kept his distance when she went right up to Gus and held out the dish of crumbs.

Gus the seagull came right over, used to their routine by now. After a few vigorous pecks, Ashley placed the dish on the ground and stepped back, watching Gus demolish the bits of bread she'd saved for him. Tom came up beside her, and she felt oddly comfortable with him, though they'd only just met.

She'd wondered what the town lawyer might be like when she'd helped her older sister settle the paperwork for their new business. Ashley was the one with the business background, and she did most of the bookkeeping for their little business. She'd liked the orderliness of the lawyer's correspondence and the clarity of his instructions. He'd laid out everything in a sensible way, which was something she'd come to learn wasn't always the case with lawyers.

She had looked forward to meeting him when they moved in, but he hadn't come by the bakery. Until now. She wondered why he'd waited so long, and why he'd chosen this odd hour and this particular day to drop by.

He seemed nervous, so she didn't press him. She had sympathy for socially shy people, since she'd been one in her younger days. It was only after she'd gotten involved in the speech and debate club in high school and developed those skills in moot court competitions in law school that she had really blossomed. She'd lost her fear of talking in front of people and was better able to handle social situations as she gained confidence.

But then all hell had broken loose soon after she took her first job, and she'd come running back home to her sisters. She was better off with them, doing something she enjoyed even more than her former profession. Law was work, but baking... That was fun.

Baking had always been her outlet, even before she had gotten serious about her education. Baking for her was creating, and she came up with a lot of the unique recipes they used in their shop. She liked spending the quiet hours before dawn beating bread dough into submission and experimenting with new flavors and textures.

She liked being in the shop alone from about four in the morning until her older sister came in to help with the breakfast rush, such as it was in this small town. Ashley left the store in Nell's capable hands after the breakfast crowd dwindled, and she had the rest of the day to herself.

"You named a seagull Gus?" Tom said quietly, picking up the question she hadn't answered on her way out of the store.

She shrugged. "Gus the gull. It seemed appropriate."

"I can't believe the rest of his flock hasn't show up to fight him for those crumbs."

"I don't think Gus really has a flock. He's

kind of a loner. And he's been living rough. See his wing?" Ashley pointed to the way some of Gus's feathers didn't quite sit right. "I've tried to get close enough to examine why it's like that, but he won't let me. I'm hoping someday we'll build enough trust up that he'll let me help him out, but for now, feeding him in the morning is all we've managed to agree upon." She sighed as she looked as closely as she could at the seagull's injuries. He'd been through the wars and had a few scars on his legs to prove it in addition the wing issue.

They watched in companionable silence while Gus finished his breakfast, then flew away.

"It doesn't seem to affect his ability to fly," Tom observed as the seagull flew off toward the water.

Ashley watched the bird go and sighed once more. "No, he can fly well enough, but something's not right there, and I'd love to see if I could help him be more comfortable."

Tom turned and she looked at him, meeting his sharp brown gaze. "You have a good heart, Ashley Baker. Not many people would care so much about a dumb animal."

"Gus isn't dumb. He's smart enough to con me out of breakfast every day." She smiled and opened the bakery door.

"Point taken," Tom said, following behind her as she went back indoors.

She didn't seek the imaginary safety of the counter. Instead, she leaned against one of the tables and turned to confront her guest.

"So, what brings you to my door this early in the morning, counselor?" She folded her arms and watched him squirm a bit before he came up with a reply.

She wasn't sure why, but it seemed she made him nervous. Imagine that.

"What makes you think I didn't just come for breakfast?" he countered, leaning on the table opposite her.

She should have expected the counter-argument. He was a lawyer, after all.

"Well, let's see. In the months since we've been open, just about every resident of the cove has been in here at least once—if only to check us out and grumble." There were a few notable curmudgeons in the area who would gladly buy their baked goods but weren't exactly friendly about it. "You, however, have never been in. Not once. I noticed."

"Why would you notice something like that, especially?" His tone challenged her. The single arched eyebrow dared her to tell him the truth. Ashley squirmed.

"If you must know, I've wanted to put a face to your name ever since we started the application process to move here. I liked your style, counselor. Your papers were precise and orderly. That's not something I've seen all that often, and I admit, I admired your work. Can you blame me for wanting to meet you?"

Tom shrugged those massive, muscled shoulders. Ashley had noticed how fit he was. Then again, most of the residents of this town were fit and what she'd call *buff*. They were shapeshifters, after all. She and her younger sister, Tina, had seen a few of them shifting into bears from their rooftop garden within the first few weeks of living there.

At first, Ashley hadn't been sure of what they were seeing, but as time went on and more men got naked in the woods behind their building, and then bears stood in their places, Ash and Tina had put two and two together, as it were. Incredible as it had seemed, they were living in a town full of bear shifters.

And then their oldest sister had gone and gotten engaged to one of them. The sheriff, a hunky guy named Brody Chambers, was a hottie, no doubt about it, and he'd be their brother-in-law in the not-too-distant future. They had been planning the wedding for the past week, ever since the happy couple had made the announcement at a dinner party at Brody's home in the woods.

Brody and Nell were supposed to break the big news about him being a shapeshifter at that dinner, but Ashley and Tina had already known. It was Nell who had been out of the loop on that big secret. The younger sisters had opted not to tell Nell until they were all well-settled into town because they didn't want their overprotective sister uprooting them. They were done moving around. The sisters liked this cove full of extraordinary beings, and they wanted to stay.

The lawyer was just as hunky as Brody. No, he was even more handsome to Ashley's mind, because not only did he have those broad shoulders, narrow hips, and muscles that showed through his clothes, he also had a demonstrated ability to use his brain. Ash had always found a man's mind as attractive as the outer packaging.

And Tom definitely had superior outer packaging to go with his orderly mind. She'd liked his style even before she'd seen him, and now that she'd finally met him, she found him very, very attractive.

"I guess your sisters let you handle the paperwork, considering your background." Tom's eyes dared her to confirm his suspicions, and they held far too much knowledge.

"You know?" She sucked in a breath, truly surprised, though she probably shouldn't have been.

"Honey," his tone dropped, turning the word into a soft endearment, "I did background checks on all of you. Big John trusts me to vet whoever we allow into our community."

She grabbed the back of a nearby chair and sat, her knees almost giving out on her because of his stunning news.

"Does everybody know?" she asked in a broken whisper.

Tom crouched before her, taking her shaking hands in his. "No. Only me. I just told John that you were okay, and he took me at my word.''

CHAPTER THREE

"I was cleared. Cleared of all charges, I mean." Her voice was weaker than she liked when she finally looked up to meet his warm brown gaze.

"I know. I looked into it. The New York press treated you badly. You did all you could for those kids. It wasn't your fault."

His strong, solemn tone touched her, even as the horror of the past that had sent her running from her big corporate job in New York with her tail between her legs came back, hitting her once more. It had been a long time since she'd been confronted by such an out-of-the-blue reminder of everything that had happened. She'd run home to her sisters, and they'd taken her in and let her join them on their next adventure.

"Then you know it all," she said, knowing

her tone was as bleak as the desolate place inside her that had been utterly destroyed by the events that had run her out of New York on a rail.

"Most of it." He stood and pulled a chair over, close to her, sitting opposite her.

He was easy to be around. He didn't rush her to speak or bombard her with questions. She liked that. But even so, she knew he expected her to say something.

"Nell and Tina already had a successful bistro in Portland. They had a regular customer who had retired to the west coast, and he got me the interview with his old firm in New York after I graduated law school. If I'd known what I was in for though, I don't think I would've done it. Hindsight is twenty-twenty, isn't it?" She had to laugh, or else she'd cry. And she didn't want to cry about this anymore. Especially not in front of this man. "So there I was, fresh out of school, full of myself and not knowing that I was as green as grass and ripe for a fall. They put me on the Hilliand case, and I did my best to follow orders and file all the motions for custody. Well, you probably saw what happened as it played out in the media. I became the public face of the law firm for

software billionaire Bob Hilliand. And I got
the blame when his ex-wife won custody of
their three little ones and whisked them off
to Slovenia. When they were killed in the
plane crash…" Her voice trailed off.

"The press hounded you, blaming you for
their deaths. If you hadn't screwed up the
paperwork, they would never have been
allowed to leave the States. Isn't that how it
went?" Tom's voice was neither accusatory
nor sympathetic.

"Something like that. But…I didn't," she
whispered. "I didn't screw up. What I filed
should have worked. When the papers were
released… That wasn't my work. Only, no
one would believe me."

"Whose was it? Do you know?" His
question was gentle but firm.

She met his gaze. "I know who it was, but
there's no way to prove it. She set me up for
the fall in order to climb right over my back
into a better position in the firm. She didn't
care about the client, at all. In fact, she
probably counted it lucky that the mother
and children died. It made me look even
worse than losing the custody battle. I left
the firm in disgrace, and her way was clear to
advance."

"People like that are the reason I hate our profession," Tom said, sitting back in his chair and blowing out a gusty sigh.

"You believe me?" Ashley searched his gaze, surprised by his open attitude after the horrible reputation she'd earned in the press.

"No reason why I shouldn't." He spread his hands on his jeans-clad thighs, and she followed the movement with her gaze. He had big hands. Rough and calloused. Not like most lawyers' hands she'd ever seen. This was a man who worked with his hands as well as his mind.

He also had a mishmash of faded paint stains on his fingers. She knew he was a painter of some renown. All the residents of Grizzly Cove did some kind of art. The place had been founded as an artists' colony, though Ash and Tina had figured out soon after moving here that a lot of the residents were also shapeshifters.

First off, most of the men didn't act like artists. They weren't flamboyant. Just tall, muscular and hunky. The place was populated mostly by men, which the sisters had discussed at length. It was a less civilized stretch of the coast, to be sure, but they were slowly bringing the comforts of small-town living to the area. The three sisters were the first outsiders they'd let in to their growing community, and there were very few females besides the three human Baker sisters.

In fact, she could count the other women in the area on one hand. There was Lyn Ling and her adorable four-year-old daughter, Daisy. Lyn made art out of bamboo, and it was said she kept a grove of the stuff growing out by her home in the woods. She was Chinese by origin, but had lost her husband and come to this town for a fresh start.

Maya Marshall was Big John's sister. She had a lovely little workshop just down the street from the bakery, where she sold the most amazing pieces of one-of-a-kind handmade jewelry. Jayne Sherman was Maya's best friend, off-and-on partner in the jewelry business and the town's only registered nurse.

The final female of note was a reclusive watercolorist named Mary MacDonnell, who came in to the bakery twice a week or so to stock up on breads and buy a few pastries. All of the ladies were likely shapeshifters of some kind, though Ash had thought it rude to ask.

Tom was probably one of the grizzly bears she and Tina had seen roaming the woods behind the bakery. He was certainly large enough. And muscular enough. She liked the look of his broad shoulders and bulging biceps.

Was it getting hot in here? She thought momentarily about the ovens in back, but the timers would beep when the bread was done. There was no beeping, just the pounding of her heart as she talked to this gorgeous hunk of man who—*saints preserve us*—seemed to be keeping an open mind where her colorful past was concerned. He was getting even more attractive, by the moment.

"Besides," he went on, blissfully unaware of her perusal, "I know when people are lying to me. I'm also a really good judge of character. So is just about everyone here. Especially our mayor. You and your sisters are okay with Big John, so that means you're okay. End of story."

"But that isn't really the end of the story, is it?" she countered, still uncomfortable that he knew her deep, dark secret. "My sisters moved here, in part, to help me start over. The press hounded me. You have no idea…" She ran a hand over her hair, feeling the sorrow and frustration of those days all over again. "It was awful."

"I won't tell anyone." His voice was reassuringly strong, though the deep tone created a sort of intimacy that warmed her.

She looked up, meeting his gaze. "How can I be sure, though? It would kill me to have to move again. I'd have to leave my sisters behind now that Nell is marrying Brody, and Tina's so infatuated with all of you people and your abilities…"

Tom actually chuckled, and Ash couldn't figure out why. She scowled at him until he held up one hand, palm outward.

"Honey, that's the reason I'm here. Big John asked me to come talk to you and your sister, to make sure you wouldn't go telling the rest of the world about *us*."

"Huh." She sat back in her chair, nonplussed. "So we both know something about the other we don't want getting out." A dark thought occurred to her. "Were you going to threaten me with exposure if I didn't keep your secret? Because if that's your game—"

"Peace, Ashley," Tom interrupted her, this time raising both hands in a gesture of surrender. "That wasn't my angle. I was simply going to ask, but I couldn't quite figure out how to do it. I wanted to get to know you a little first, and see what you were like. I should've come in when you first moved to town, like everybody else did, to check you and your sisters out, but...well...I didn't. I'm sorry for that now." He smiled at her, and she was glad she was sitting down. His smile packed a wallop. "Truce?"

How could she say no when the handsomest man she'd ever met looked at her with those puppy-dog eyes and asked so nicely? She couldn't help herself. She caved.

"Okay. Truce." She reached out to shake the hand he offered. "I won't tell if you won't."

Something almost electric passed between them as she touched his hand. He held hers for longer than strictly necessary, and her breath hitched. Time seemed to spin out, stretching as she looked deep into those stunning brown eyes of his...

And then he let go. At least she had the satisfaction of realizing that he seemed as shaken as she was by the strange moment. His eyes gave him away. They held a trace of the same confusion she was feeling, along with a sort of wonder that made her breath catch again.

This man had the most amazing effect on her.

Beep. Beep. Beep.

"I think your oven is calling." Tom grinned at her.

"What?" She shook her head to break the daze she seemed to have fallen into. "Oh!" Ashley ran around the counter and saved the bread, moving pans around while keeping one eye on Tom, to make sure he wasn't going to just leave without saying goodbye.

She put the bread onto the cooling racks and loaded the next batch, which she'd already prepared before he came in. Task done, she wiped her hands as she went back up front. He was still there. Just on the other side of the counter.

"That bread smells really amazing," he offered, looking over her head at the cooling racks that were just visible behind her.

"Thanks. Want some?" She motioned with her chin back toward the bread.

"Yeah, I could take some to go, I guess."

Oh. He had to leave. Why did her heart sink at the thought?

"There's just one more thing." He looked

kind of hesitant to speak, and that intrigued her.

Ashley's heart went pitter-pat wondering what the one-more-thing could be? Would it be something personal? Would he ask her out? She felt…sort of…giddy. Yeah, that's what it was. Giddiness.

When was the last time Ashley Baker, disgraced lawyer and therapeutic baker, had felt giddy? She couldn't even remember, and that struck her as kind of sad. Yet, here was a man who made her feel things she hadn't felt in a very long time. Things were looking up—as long as he stuck around.

"What is it?" she asked, unwilling to wait for him to get around to speaking again.

"It's your sister."

Hmm. Her heart sank a little.

"Which one?"

His answer to that question was key. If he was asking about Nell, no problem. Nell was happily engaged. But if he was asking after pretty, younger, gets-all-the-boys Tina…

"Tina."

There it went. Her hopeful, foolish heart hit the dirt.

"What about her?" Ashley stood strong, not letting her disappointment show. She hoped.

"Well, I don't know her. How can I be sure she won't go blogging about *Grizzly Cove, Home of the Rare Bear Shapeshifters* or something?" Tom diffused his tough words with a charming grin that Ashley fought against. She refused to be charmed by another guy who might just be using her to get to her sister. "Can she be trusted?"

Wait. Was he asking Ashley's opinion? Did he not want an introduction to Tina to find out for himself?

"Tina's always been trustworthy. She doesn't tell tales, and she doesn't have a blog." Ashley chuckled at the thought. "My sisters have sort of rallied around me since I came home with my tail tucked between my legs. They mostly stay off social media and try to run under the radar for my sake. It's old news now, but every once in a while, when we were still in Portland, some enterprising reporter would jump out at me from the bushes, or try to get to me through my sisters on the internet. Since then, they've pretty much closed ranks to protect me. I don't think Tina would seek attention from anyone in the media, lest it somehow bounce back on me again. She wouldn't do that to me. We moved this far to get away from my past. Tina wouldn't ruin that. She likes it here."

Ashley wouldn't tell him how much Tina enjoyed spying on the hunky guys who dropped trou in the woods and turned into bears. It had become a bit of a sport for her to sit up on the roof and try to spot them. That was about as exciting as things got around here, after all.

Moving up here had been hardest on Tina, but she never complained. She'd had an active social life back in Portland, though no serious boyfriends. Not any that lasted longer than a few months, at any rate.

"I trust your judgment, but I'd still like to talk with her," Tom said, depressing Ashley further.

Maybe he *was* interested in her younger sister. Ashley wouldn't be surprised. It had happened before. Quite a few times, in fact.

"She works the night shift," Ashley replied in as bland a tone as she could manage.

"Yeah, I know, but..." He trailed off, and she became intrigued despite her better judgment. "Will you be here tonight too?"

Ashley dusted off the non-dusty counter

with her towel. "There's no reason to fear Tina. She's harmless. You're a big boy. You can introduce yourself."

"Oh. Well, yeah," he agreed quickly, seeming somewhat surprised by her brusque answer. "But I was hoping to see *you* again. I mean, I'd like to talk to Tina, just to be sure, but I was wondering if maybe you'd like to have dinner with me."

CHAPTER FOUR

For a lawyer, he wasn't all that eloquent.

And there went her heart again, going pitter-pat. Had he really just asked her out?

"Since this is the only place to eat in town, at the moment, I thought maybe I could meet you here, then talk to your sister before we grab a bite and then maybe take a walk on the beach after?" He seemed nervous, talking quickly when she didn't answer right away.

Damn. He really did just ask her out. Her. Not Tina. Inside, Ashley raised a mental fist in victory.

"How about we meet here and you can talk to Tina, but then, maybe instead of eating in here, could I offer you the setting of our rooftop garden? It's really pretty up there. We strung white twinkle lights among the flower pots, and we sit up there at night

33

sometimes, and stargaze."

Was she talking too much? It felt like maybe she was. Ashley stuttered to a halt and waited to see what he'd say.

He gave her one of those electrifying grins that made her knees wobble. "I'd like that very much. What time is good for you?"

She wanted to say right now, but it wasn't even eight o'clock in the morning. She'd have all day to prep and worry and try to get ready.

"Is seven too late?" She picked a time she knew Tina would be the least busy.

If needs be, Ash could take over for a few minutes while Tom talked to Tina. Seven was right in between the dinner crowd and the folks who strolled in for latte and dessert.

Tom's smile widened. "Seven is perfect. I'll look forward to seeing you then."

"Me too." Not a witty answer, but it was the best she could do under the circumstances. Tom's smiles made her feel all warm inside, and they sort of melted a part of her brain—the thinking part, no doubt.

She jumped, realizing he was probably waiting for her to get the bread they'd talked about a minute ago. She went back and quickly selected one of the best loaves, packaging it in the special bags they'd had printed, that were both long and wide enough for the special shapes Ashley liked to make. She handed him the still-warm bread across the counter.

"This one's on the house. Hope you like it. It's honey walnut." She felt a little shy all of a sudden. Should she have given him one of the plainer selections?

"Sounds delicious. You know, we bears love honey. And I am particularly fond of walnuts." He brushed her hand with his as he took the loaf from her, and she swore she could feel little sparks against her skin, like little zaps of static electricity. "Thank you, Ashley."

His warm, deep voice made a meal of her name. She liked the way he said it.

He stood there for a moment, gazing at her from across the counter, and then, he sort of shook himself and headed for the door. It looked to her like maybe he was reluctant to leave, which made her feel all tingly. Maybe he was as attracted to her as she was to him? Could she be so lucky? Well, he had just asked her out—sort of.

There wasn't much night life in the cove, so his suggestion about sharing a meal—even if it was in her family's establishment—pretty much made it a date. Ashley felt that giddiness again. She hadn't been on a date since all the trouble started back in New York.

She watched him walk away, noticing again what a fine backside he had. These shifters were built to last, every single one of them, but Tom seemed to have that little extra sex appeal that made her want to jump his bones. Not that good girl Ashley had ever really gotten wild enough with a man to jump him. Still, Tom made her think about it. Very seriously.

The bell above the door tinkled as he left, and Ashley sighed, watching him walk down the street. The town lawyer really had a great ass.

* * *

Tom was prompt, which was a good thing for Ashley's nerves. She'd frittered around the apartment upstairs all day, cleaning, setting up the table in the rooftop garden, and figuring out what to wear. As a result, her entire wardrobe was now scattered all over her room, but the little garden had been weeded and pruned until every leaf shone.

She'd been hanging around downstairs in the bakery for the past half hour, chatting idly with Tina and helping out here and there. The dinner rush—which only consisted of about a half dozen people that night—had come and mostly gone. And then, there he was. The man himself walked in the door.

He seemed only to glance at Tina before his gaze met Ashley's.

Tom saw Ashley standing there, and every other thought went straight out of his head. His inner bear liked what it saw, which was a first. Never before had his other half weighed in this strongly about a female.

He walked straight up to her, but social convention barred him from doing what he really wanted to do, so he settled for smiling at her and saying hello. If they hadn't been in public, he might've given into his baser instincts and pulled her into his arms, greeting her with a kiss…or more. Whatever she'd let him get away with. As it was, he had to be polite and make conversation, which wasn't exactly his strong suit.

"You look great," he said, knowing it wasn't polished, but at least it was true.

"Thanks." Her smile lit his world, and he was glad he'd opted to speak the first thoughts that jumped into his head. "You too." A throat cleared nearby, and Ashley jumped. "Sorry. Tom, this is my sister, Tina. Tina, this is Tom."

The younger sister stuck her hand over the counter and gave Tom a speculative smile as she looked from him to Ashley and back again. He shook Tina's hand, but there was no spark. Not like when he touched Ashley.

So it wasn't a Baker sister thing. It was just an Ashley thing. Good to know.

"You're the town's lawyer, right?" Tina asked, letting go of his hand.

"Yeah, that's me," he agreed.

"Ash said you wanted to talk to me?" Tina went on. "Don't worry, your secret's safe with me. Nell read me the riot act already, but it wasn't necessary. I get that you guys have a good thing going here, and I won't ruin it for you—or for my sisters. Are we cool?"

Tom's head was spinning a bit by the speed of Tina's words, but his inner bear scented the absolute truth in her words. There wasn't much guile in this young woman. Tom's built-in lie detector knew she was on the level, even if she left his human side in a whirl.

"Yeah," he said, his human thought processes catching up with his bear's instincts. "I think we're cool. I can tell you don't intend to make trouble for us, and most especially for your family." Tom decided to take it a step further. "You know, now that Nell is part of the Clan by mating with Brody, you two are under our protection too. If you ever have any trouble, you just come to me, or better yet, go to John. He looks out for all of us. He's the man in charge. Our Alpha. Did Brody explain about that?"

"You mean he's leader of the pack, right?" Tina said offhandedly.

"Packs are for wolves. We're bears. We call our groupings Clans," Tom told her.

"Wolves?" Ashley piped up, sounding surprised. "You mean there are people who turn into wolves too?"

"Duh," Tina intoned before Tom could

say anything. "Where do you think the legends about werewolves come from, Ash? Seriously." Tina shook her head as she wiped the counter with a dish towel.

Ashley blushed rather becomingly, Tom thought. He decided to tell her a bit more about the world the sisters now found themselves in.

"Wolves, big cats, raptors. There are all sorts of shapeshifters, each with their own hierarchy. But we all answer to the Lords."

"Like nobility?" Ash asked him, then turned to her sister. "There's shapeshifter nobility?"

"Sort of, but it's not a hereditary title. The Lords are always twin Alphas, and the duty usually falls to a different group in each generation. The current Lords of North America are wolves, but we've heard rumors that the next generation will be from a bear Clan." Tom felt a swell of pride knowing that the next Lords would be bears.

"How do they decide which group gets the leadership? Is there a vote or something?" Tina asked.

Tom shook his head. "No. No voting. Identical twins are rare among shifters. When a set is born, we know the Mother of

All has chosen them to be the next Lords." That's just the way it was. The way it had always been.

"Mother of All? Is that like Mother Nature or something?" Tina asked.

"The Goddess has many names and many guises. I know most of your human religions feature a male deity, but shifters have served the Goddess for as long as there have been shifters."

"Wow," Tina commented. "Progressive."

The bell above the door jingled and Tina went over to assist the newcomers. It was Lyn and her daughter, Daisy. Though most four-year-olds would be going to sleep soon, shifter kids had a bit more energy than their human counterparts, so it looked like mother and daughter had come in for dessert.

CHAPTER FIVE

"Shall we go upstairs?" Ashley asked after greetings had been exchanged.

"Lead the way," Tom answered, knowing he was smiling and unable to stop himself.

He hadn't been on a date in way too long, and he'd never really experimented with human women. There was something so incredibly alluring about Ashley though...something primal that demanded he get closer to her.

Tom followed Ashley through a door marked *private*, up a flight of stairs and into a cozy apartment that took up the entire top floor of the building. Everything up here was feminine, with soft edges and colors. It was nice, Tom thought, though his own taste ran more toward hunter green and navy blue.

She kept going, leading him to another set of stairs that took them onto the roof. Tom followed, bemused by what he found up there. The sisters had turned a plain, flat roof into an oasis in the middle of the village. There were planters of every size and shape—most made of wood that the ladies must have built themselves—all over the roof. In the center was a patio table that had been set with silverware and china. In the center of the table, a thermal bag held something warm that Tom could scent was some kind of beef.

A green salad with tomatoes sat under a net cover, and a small rack of condiments lay nearby. Ashley had gone all out, and Tom was duly impressed, though he also felt a little guilty.

"I didn't mean to make you go through all this trouble, but it looks great, and the food smells great." He looked at the views in the early evening light. "This is really nice up here."

"It's our little getaway. We spend a lot of time up here, tending the plants and just enjoying the sunny days." She led him toward the table in the center of their magical garden. Fairy lights were woven throughout the planters, lighting the path with a soft illumination.

The salad, Tom learned, had come fresh from the garden, as had most of the vegetables and herbs. Tom admired the sisters' ingenuity in growing their own fresh produce in a town that didn't really have much in the way of groceries. Some of the shops stocked various meats, and there was a fresh fish market, but getting fresh lettuce, for one example, wasn't a high priority for most in the town.

Ashley had made a roast that was cooked to perfection. Some kind of herbed potato dish went with it, along with the salad and a green bean dish that was absolutely delicious. Tom complimented her cooking many times throughout the meal.

"I didn't mean for you to go to all this trouble, but it was fantastic," Tom said, as they finished the meal. "Thank you. Next time, I'm going to cook for you." He gathered his courage, knowing his inner bear wouldn't allow him to wait. This woman was too special. "In fact, how about tomorrow? I can pick you up and bring you out to my place. I've got a huge grill, and I've even been known to marinate a steak or two in my time."

"Really? Do tell." Her answer was flirty.

Tom took it as a good sign.

"I even have the beginnings of a small wine cellar," he told her with a knowing nod as he raised his glass to her. She'd paired the roast with a very nice red wine that he truly appreciated. Wine was one of his little hobbies.

"I'm impressed. Are you going to offer to show me your etchings next?" She was still flirting with him. A tiny bubble of joy rose up from the center of his being. He couldn't remember having this much fun with anyone in a good, long time.

"No etchings, but I do have a studio overlooking the cove. In fact…" he said, getting excited as he looked at the view from the rooftop, "I'd love to paint the cove from up here sometime. It's a unique perspective, and the light is phenomenal."

They'd moved to sit on a bench the sisters had placed at the front of the roof where they could look out over the cove. The dusk had given way to dark, and the only illumination was the soft twinkle of the fairy lights in the garden behind them, the dusting of stars and quarter moon overhead, and the occasional flutter of the lights from a ship out at sea.

The cove itself wasn't large or deep enough for any serious docks. There were a few small boats, at least one of which was used exclusively for fishing by the same shifter who owned the fish market. He supplied everyone who didn't want to do their own fishing. The other boats belonged to various residents who enjoyed occasional sport fishing or just sailing along the coast.

"You could," Ashley said softly. "I mean, I don't think my sisters would mind if you wanted to use our garden as your studio for a little while. I've seen some of your work in the gallery next door, and it's very powerful."

She'd seen his art? And liked it? That touched him more than he thought it would.

"I never really painted much before coming here," he admitted. "But I've discovered a passion for it." He had to laugh. "I thought John's idea of disguising ourselves as artists was a little nuts at first, but the man has vision. A lot of us have discovered hidden talents and a real joy in creating things. It's somewhat therapeutic, and while my inner bear doesn't truly understand the point of it all, it does appreciate beauty. Painting calms the beast a bit, which is a nice added benefit. Having so many of us living in such close proximity could have been disastrous otherwise. Usually, we don't group together like a lot of other shifters do. Mostly we just have our small family units as part of a larger Clan that we see every once in a while, but we don't all live together in the same place."

"So this place is a sort of social experiment," Ashley mused.

"In more than one way," Tom agreed. "John's also managed to turn us all into artists. That was a pretty massive undertaking in itself. I honestly thought—if anything—we'd have an entire community of chainsaw carvers."

Ashley laughed, and the sound warmed Tom's soul. There was something so enchanting about this woman, and he wanted to get closer to her.

Trying out one of his rusty moves, he put his arm along the back of the bench, behind her. When she didn't object, he relaxed, enjoying her nearness.

"Brody carves with a chainsaw," she said quietly, her tone amused as she moved closer and practically snuggled into his side.

"Don't get me wrong; I like your sister's mate. Brody and I go way back. But applying the term *art* to those tree stumps he attacks with a chainsaw isn't something I care to do. Besides, all he does are self-portraits." Tom liked being close to Ashley. She smelled divine, and his inner bear grumbled happily in the back of his mind.

"He does seem to carve a lot of bears," she allowed.

"Look closer. They're all the *same* bear."

She chuckled, and he felt a small sense of triumph that he'd been able to make her laugh. Brody's ongoing series of self-portraits had become something of a running joke within the Clan.

"Just think of all those poor, ignorant tourists, totally unaware that they're stuck with a self-portrait of your brother-in-law on their front lawn."

This time, she laughed outright. Tom liked making her laugh. He enjoyed the cheerful tones of her amusement and the way her eyes lit up.

Unable to let the moment pass, Tom followed his instincts and leaned over to cover her smiling lips with his. Their first kiss, and it was one of joy.

It quickly turned into something much sultrier as she turned into his arms, and he drew her against his body. She tasted of the peppery wine they'd had with dinner and her own unique essence. He couldn't get enough.

Tom's inner bear wanted to lick her all over and learn her different tastes, but it was too soon for that. He counseled the grizzly to patience while his human form got to know her responses, cataloging each one and learning what made her tremble.

Her passion was as quick to ignite as his, which was good. It meant they were a good match, and that she was as attracted to him as he was to her. So far, so good.

Tom lifted her legs so they stretched across his lap. She let him move her around to suit his mood, her cooperation making him want to growl in victory. She was with him. She was part of this seduction, this initiation, this getting to know each other.

Her tiny hands roamed over his back and then his shoulders and arms, learning him, testing the feel of his muscles against her fingers. He damned the cloth that separated his skin from her touch, but he had to be patient. She was human. He had to let things progress at a slower pace. He didn't want to scare her off.

She was quickly becoming much too important to him for him to mess this up. He told himself again, to be patient. And when she pushed eagerly at his clothing, he wanted to go with her instincts and get them both naked on the roof, under the stars.

But he heard noises in the apartment below. It was late. Tina had closed the bakery and was making a lot of noise— probably to give them fair warning that she was in the apartment.

It was time to end their first date, even though he didn't want to go. Not now. But he had to.

Reluctantly, he caught her fingers and stilled her movements, ending their kisses.

"I've got to go," he said, hating every word, but knowing it was the right thing. For now. "But I want to see you again. Are we still on for tomorrow? My place? I'll pick you up."

He held her hands gently between his own, raising them to place little kisses on her fingertips. He couldn't help himself. If she was near, he wanted to touch her. To kiss her.

A bang came from downstairs, loud enough for Ashley to hear.

"Damn, it must be later than I realized," she said, blushing prettily now that the dazed confusion was slowly leaving her gaze. He liked that he'd put that dreamy expression on her face. "Tina's downstairs."

"I know." He kissed her knuckles gently. "That's why I stopped us from going any further."

She blushed even more. Tom could see it in the faint light. His night vision was pretty good. And her response made him want to cuddle her.

"I'm glad one of us kept a level head," she muttered as she allowed him to hug her against his chest. Her head fit nicely into the crook of his neck, as if made to belong there. To belong to him, and him alone.

"I will always protect you, Ashley. In every situation. It's part of my instincts. Hard-wired, if you will." He rubbed his hand down her arm from shoulder to wrist and back again in soothing motions. He loved touching her.

"You know, that could sound stalker-ish, but I find it comforting. I feel like I've known you a lot longer than just a day." Her words slipped quietly into the evening breeze, and straight into his heart.

"I feel the same way, honey. Sometimes it happens like that for my kind. Courtships can be a bit...accelerated. But I give you my word, I will try my best not rush you."

She eased from his arms and sat on the bench next to him, then she met his gaze. "Is that what we're doing? Beginning a courtship?"

Tom took a deep breath, gathering his courage before answering. "I'd like to think so. If you're okay with that. We call it the mating dance."

She looked out over the cove, then up at the stars before answering. "Yeah, I think I'm okay with it. I like you, Tom. That's a good first step."

She stood and walked to the table, gathering the plates and putting them in a plastic caddy she'd had stowed to one side. He helped her clean up, prolonging the moments he had with her, but it didn't take long to put the roof garden back to rights.

Together, they went back down into the apartment after shutting off the little lights on the roof. Tina was nowhere in evidence, but they both knew she was somewhere in the apartment. They dropped the dishes off near the sink, and Ashley motioned for him to follow her down the stairs that led into the bakery.

He kissed her again—a long, lingering but all-too-chaste kiss—in the door of the closed bakery, and then, he left, heading for home. They'd made a start. And for that, Tom sent a little prayer of thanks heavenward to the Mother of All.

He wasn't one hundred percent sure yet, but he had a good feeling that Ashley Baker might just be his mate.

CHAPTER SIX

Tom couldn't stay away. After a mostly sleepless night, he found himself at the bakery bright and early, when only Ashley was there. She welcomed him with a smile, and they shared a quiet breakfast while her bread baked.

They even went outside to watch the sunrise and to feed Gus, the seagull. Little things that were becoming rituals after only two days with her. Tom wanted to spend every moment with Ashley, but he couldn't. For one thing, he had promised John he would work on some permits from the state today. For another, he had to prepare for their date. He'd promised to cook for her, and he had to get some supplies and clean his house a bit.

He left her as the morning customers started coming in and her sister joined her behind the counter. He didn't try to kiss her. Not in public. Not with their relationship so new. He didn't want to make her feel uncomfortable, but he was definitely making plans for kissing her—and whatever else she would allow him to do—at his place tonight.

He couldn't wait.

By the time dinner rolled around, Asheley was a nervous wreck. She'd showered and primped, shaving and putting lotion on every part of her skin she could reasonably reach. She'd given herself a mani/pedi and spent almost an hour on her hair.

The entire contents of her wardrobe was strewn all over her room again, but that seemed to be the norm now for preparing for a date with Tom. He'd left her at the bakery this morning, and she'd practically waltzed through the rest of her shift, her feet barely touching the ground.

It had been a long time since the mere prospect of a date with a man had made her that happy, and she intended to savor it. Almost as much as she intended to jump his bones tonight if the opportunity arose.

Tom drove up to the bakery and parked in front. He was driving a Jeep with the top

BIANCA D'ARC

down and looked absolutely scrumptious.
Ashley stood in front of the display case,
fighting the urge to step up to the door. It
wouldn't do to let him see how eager she
was, would it?

Tina came up beside her, folding her
arms as she leaned against the case beside
Ashley. The bakery was quiet for the
moment, though a few of the locals were
sitting outside at one of the tables they'd
been able to set up on the sidewalk in front
of the shop. They all seemed to stop and
look when Tom pulled up.

Ashley noticed the way the men greeted
Tom with nods of respect, but Tom didn't
stop to chat. He had a rather intense look on
his face that matched the way Ashley was
feeling.

"He looks good enough to eat," Tina
commented as they both watched Tom walk
toward the door.

"Hush," Ashley chastised her sister.

"Well, he does," Tina protested. "I'm just
sayin'…"

Thankfully, Tina didn't say anything more
as Tom opened the door and the bell over it
jangled. He strode in, and Ashley's mouth
went dry. He really was the most handsome

man she'd ever seen in person. Certainly the nicest—both in looks and personality—she'd ever been on a date with.

Tom walked right up to her, a smile stretching his face. "Hi," he said, meeting and holding her gaze.

"Hi," Ashley replied in a breathy tone.

"Well," Tina's loud voice intruded on the moment. "It's good to see you again, counselor."

"Good to see you too, Tina." Tom seemed to have trouble tearing his gaze away from Ash to acknowledge Tina's greeting.

Tina chuckled and flounced away, clearly amused at them, but Ashley was just glad to see her go.

"Are you ready to go?" Tom asked.

"Yeah, just let me grab one thing," Ashley turned around to find Tina standing behind her, holding up the box of pastries she'd put together earlier.

She and Tom walked out together, Tina snickering behind them, but Ashley didn't care. She felt like Cinderella being picked up by Prince Charming, in the pumpkin coach, heading for the ball.

The locals at the table outside gave them speculative looks as they passed but didn't say anything. Ashley wasn't sure what they thought about another of their kind dating a human, but so far, the response to Brody and Nell's relationship had been mostly positive.

Tom helped her hop into the vehicle then jogged around to the driver's side and got in. Within moments, they had left the small Main Street behind and were out on the back roads that led around the side of the cove.

Tom's home was set a short distance from the shore, on a high point in the terrain that would afford some protection if the tide rose during a storm or something. It was a beautiful structure, with numerous tall windows that probably let in lots of light during the day. As it was, in the early evening twilight, Ashley got to see the beautiful views Tom had of the cove as the sun set in the west, turning the waters all sorts of vibrant colors.

"This place is just lovely," Ashley complimented his home as they walked in, and she got a good look at the floor-to-ceiling windows that showcased the natural beauty of the cove.

"Thanks. I designed it around the views, and my studio is all about the light." He led the way around, showing her each of the rooms on the main floor. The house had a mostly open floor plan, so the tour didn't take very long.

She was impressed by everything she saw, but when he led the way into his studio, her breath caught.

On an easel in the center of the room was a massive canvas that looked nearly finished. It was a view of the cove at sunset with the vibrant colors of the dying sun reflected off tempestuous waves. The piece spoke of the power of nature and the majesty of their surroundings. Its subject matter was rugged, and yet, the painting was refined in its technique. It was a masterpiece.

"Oh, wow. Tom, this is brilliant." She moved into the room, drawn by the beauty of the image.

"John asked me to do something for the new town hall he's building. This will hang across from the front entrance, so you see it when you walk in."

"It's magnificent." She stood, just admiring the big canvas for a while. "It looks alive. I can almost feel the motion of the waves." She looked at Tom. "You're really talented."

He seemed almost uncomfortable with her praise but gave her a gruff thank you before bringing her attention to the skylights he'd installed. He also pointed out the array of windows that he claimed brought in all kinds of light during different parts of the day. Light, apparently, was very significant to painters, which Ashley had known in a sort of abstract way but was becoming much more educated about as he expounded on the virtues and drawbacks of the light at different times of the day.

She saw a few more of his canvases, propped up around the room. Several were drying, he said, in preparation for being moved to the gallery in town. And a few more were being held aside for a showing at one of the exclusive little galleries in Portland.

"We had the gallery owner come through town on his way back from a fishing trip, and he asked several of us to exhibit," Tom told her, downplaying his part in the event.

"I heard about it from Lyn. And Nell sent the guy off with a box full of pastries. He talked to her the whole time he was in the bakery about the art in the town. He was really enthusiastic, she said." Ashley remembered the incident, which had happened just after the bakery was finally up and running smoothly, about a month after they'd moved to town.

They talked about the upcoming show and their reluctance to draw too much attention to the town. John had finally agreed to the showing as long as the gallery owner kept silent about where the artists lived. John was willing to entertain the occasional tourist in their new community, but they didn't want to attract people who might want to take up permanent residence—or worse, reporters wanting to do a story about where the artists lived.

Tom and several of the others were going to drive down to Portland for the opening, and they would make sure nobody asked too many questions about where they came from. The gallery owner would rake in his commissions, as long as he kept mum about where he'd found the art. At least until the town was better established and they'd gained experience dealing with humans and hiding in plain sight as a group.

"Are we ready for dinner?" Tom asked as his short tour came to an end.

He'd led her onto the patio, off to one

side of the house. It was screened by the forest in back, the house on the right, but most of the left side, and the entire front, faced the water. Again, the view was breathtaking.

"How far are you from town? Less than a mile or so, right?" Ashley asked, to make conversation as he busied himself starting the enormous grill.

"Just under a mile. I wanted this view in particular, so when we were figuring out who would live where, the guys let me have it. Most of them wanted to be farther into the forest, anyway, but a few of us like the water more than others." He looked up and pointed to the left, farther up the cove toward the ocean. "Drew lives next door that way. You can usually see his boat at the little dock he built, but I guess he's out late tonight. Sometimes, he stays out on the water fishing for days when the weather is nice. On the other side, back toward town, is Sven's place. His home is practically right on the beach but well hidden. He's a polar bear, so he loves the water, but John wanted him closer to the center of town because he's our only doctor. The beach house was the compromise."

"You sound like you've all known each other a long time," Ashley observed.

"Yeah, we have. Most of us congregated around John when we served in the military. John's always been more Alpha than any of us, and he was a great squad leader. The man has a strategic mind, and he thinks so far outside the box, you can't even see the box from where he is. This whole artists' colony concept was his idea. You should've heard the grumbling when he first proposed it, but he sold us on it, and here we are. It's working. And I really think it will work for years to come. We can finally settle down, stop fighting our way across the globe, and start living."

"I had no idea you had served." Ashley was impressed. She had a great respect for any person who gave of themselves to help protect others.

"We don't talk about it much. We're retired. We've put all that behind us now. The squad was sick of combat by the end. We'd put in too many years fighting human wars in faraway lands. Plus, we had about reached our limit for fooling folks. See, shifters don't age the same way you humans do. We live a lot longer."

"How much longer?" she asked quickly. "What about Nell and Brody? Is he going to stay young while she ages?"

The stricken look on her face made him answer quickly. "No, honey. Don't worry about your sister. She is Brody's true mate. The magic that makes us able to shift will also make it so that they grow old together— and Brody's rate of aging. So your sister has a very long, happy life ahead of her." She still seemed skeptical. "As for how long that could be, well, Brody's about my age now, so maybe another century or two. That's about all we'll get. We're not immortal, like the fey or the bloodletters."

"Fey?" she repeated, looking stunned. "Bloodletters?"

"Fey are about what you'd expect. Beings from another realm where magic is a way of life, not just an exception to the rule, like it is here. And bloodletters are what vampires like to be called. They usually don't like the word undead, so I'd avoid that if you ever run into one."

"Vampires are real?" Ashley looked shocked. Adorably so. Then she shook her head. "What am I saying? I'm talking to a guy who can turn into a bear, for crying out loud."

CHAPTER SEVEN

Tom thought, all in all, Ashley was taking everything rather well, but he definitely didn't want to overwhelm her with new information about the world she was just coming to understand. There would be time for her to come to terms with it all. At least he hoped she would stay with him long enough for her to get comfortable with the truth about this brave new world she had stumbled into.

Deciding a change of topic was in order, he led the way back into the house. The grill was warming up. It was time to bring out the meat.

Ashley helped him retrieve the platters he'd stashed in the fridge the night before. He had marinated some steaks overnight, as well as a platter of chicken.

"I wasn't sure what you liked best, so I

figured I couldn't go wrong with a little variety," he explained.

"This is great. It all looks delicious." She helped him carry things back outside, and they worked together as if they'd done so a million times before.

Ashley was comfortable to be with, yet her mere presence stimulated his senses in ways that made him think of long-term togetherness and commitment. He'd never thought of such things before with any other female, which argued for the fact that she might just be his mate.

He figured he'd know for sure after they made love. If his bear was still on board the Ashley forever train after that, then there was no doubt about it. They were meant to be.

There was a large round wooden table at the center of the patio, with a few cushioned chairs around it. Ashley set the table and arranged the condiments they'd brought out. She also poured the wine and brought him a glass as he stood over the grill.

"To a lovely evening," she said, raising her glass to chime with his.

"To a lovely companion," he echoed, holding her gaze as they sipped the wine.

He'd pulled out one of the special bottles for this evening.

Ashley's eyes widened when she tasted the vintage. "Oh," she exclaimed softly. "This is delicious."

"Remember those vampires I was telling you about?" Tom put his glass down so he could attend to the chicken, flipping it expertly with his tongs. "The only thing they can actually ingest is wine. It has healing properties for them, so they say. As a result, some of the best vintners in the world have been perfecting their craft for a few centuries, if you know what I mean." He gave her an exaggerated wink that made her smile.

He flicked on a small radio, and soft music spilled out. Setting her wine glass down, he took her into his arms and began dancing around the patio in a slow, swaying rhythm.

"You like wine?" Ashley asked in a tone that was casual, but the question seemed important to her.

"I do. You saw the wine fridge in the kitchen, right? I have a little bit of a wine cellar under construction right now. Every season, my colleague at the Maxwell winery sends me a few cases of their best."

"A colleague?" Ashley seemed intrigued. Tom liked that she was interested in his life.

"Their lawyer is some kind of big cat shifter. I helped her out a few times after she graduated from law school, since there are only a few of us who are both shifters and attorneys. We all know each other, and help out where we can. This girl, though, she was practically raised by vampires. She doesn't know much about shifters, but we worked together via email a time or two, and for that, her boss put me on the VIP list when he found out I truly appreciated his work. Maxwell's is one of the finest wineries in the States, and Maxwell has been at his craft for a very long time."

"Seems so odd to be talking about vampires working in actual businesses. In fiction, they're all mega-rich and don't ever have to work."

"Oh, Maxwell is mega-rich too. He's had centuries to amass his fortune, but the money has to come from somewhere and has to go somewhere too. If he just rested on his laurels, with the rate of inflation, he'd be broke in no time flat. Like anybody else, he has to make his money work for him. In his case, he puts it to work doing something he enjoys and can actually benefit from himself. It's a good situation for him."

"You sound like you admire the man," Ashley observed.

"I do," Tom admitted. "I only met him once, but he's a very charismatic fellow. Personable. Even friendly, after a fashion. We talked wines after the business part of our meeting was over, and I hear he's experimenting with bringing shifters in to work in his vineyard. He's not a snob. He treats people fairly and seems willing to try new things."

"A paragon," Ashley agreed wryly. "For someone who drinks blood."

Tom laughed outright at that. Ashley had a dry sense of humor he was only just beginning to discover. He liked it. Just as he liked pretty much everything about her.

He spun her around, back toward the grill. He dipped her, stealing a quick kiss before letting her go. It was time to tend the meat on the grill, or else they'd be eating charcoal.

She retrieved her wine glass and sat at the table, watching him cook. Everything was nearly done, so it wouldn't be long now.

They shared a companionable dinner, discussing topics ranging from wine to art to politics and religion. Tom liked the way Ashley asked what she wanted to know directly. She'd learned from her sister's mating with Brody that shifters worshiped and served the Goddess, and he was gratified by the open mind she kept when he explained a bit more about his beliefs. She wasn't rejecting anything right off the bat, which boded well for the future.

When time came for dessert, Ashley unpacked the bakery box she'd brought with her. Honey buns and other delicacies the bakery had become known for came out of the box, and Tom wasn't above devouring two of the pastries in short order. Ashley laughed at him as he licked sticky honey off his fingers, but he didn't mind.

"I guess it's true about bears and honey," she observed, watching him with a little flare of heat in her gaze that made him sit up and take notice. His inner bear was ready to get on with the rest of the evening—especially if it included shared pleasure with the enticing female sitting across from him.

"Oh, it is most definitely true. Just about everyone in town loves honey—except maybe Sven. Polar bears are weird." She laughed as he finished licking his fingers. "One of the main factors in favor of your business was the box of samples you brought when you made your presentation to the town council. The fact that you used natural ingredients—including a lot more honey than most commercial bakeries—is what sold everyone who tasted those first samples."

"So, honey was our ticket into town, eh? Tina will get a kick out of that. She's the one who first started tweaking our recipes and led us down the back-to-nature path. She'd have us go totally organic, if we let her, but the costs are just too high right now to make it worthwhile." Ashley began gathering the used plates together, naturally organizing things to take back inside. "Tina's the one who came up with the idea for our roof garden too. We all helped build it, but it was her idea. It's been great for us. Saves us money on produce, and considering how far off the beaten path this town is, it's allowed us to have fresh greens whenever we want them rather than whenever the delivery truck shows up."

"Yeah, not many of us are salad lovers,"

Tom admitted. "So, we didn't place that high a priority on that sort of thing. We all can hunt our own game, though we can also have beef and chicken delivered. Just like my wine. We pool orders and have a truck drop off a whole load every couple of months. Everybody's got a big freezer to stash their supply."

"I heard someone was starting up a ranch up the mountain that is supposed to be able to supply the town with chicken, turkey, pork, beef and even bison, eventually," she said as they worked together to clear the table, moving in and out of the patio doors, brushing each other from time to time as they carried things.

Tom's mind wasn't really on the conversation. He was thinking more about what would come next. Was she cleaning up in preparation for leaving? Or was she cleaning up because she was just a neat person who wanted to have everything in order before they sat and drank more wine…and maybe did other things? Tom was eager to find out.

"Yeah, that's the plan, but it'll be a while down the road yet. Livestock tends to be nervous around us, so we're looking into outsourcing the labor, but every applicant has to be vetted. As we learned from you and your sisters, we're not very good at keeping our secret yet. We have to be careful who we allow access to our town."

"I'm surprised you have such control. I mean, I thought people could come and go wherever they wanted in the U.S."

"Technically, we're only partly in the U.S.," Tom explained. "Much of our land is on the outskirts of the reservation. We have a good relationship with the elders, and they know we are excellent stewards of the land. Native Americans are some of the only humans who are raised to believe in us. The local shaman knows what we are, and he trusts us to do right by the land, and by their people. In fact, that ranch will probably employ a large number of the tribe's younger folk, when it finally gets up and running. We have a few other irons in the fire to create employment opportunities, and the tribe gets a percentage of our art sales. It's our way of giving back to their community, since they welcomed us so warmly. We're even looking at constructing a new building on Main Street for the tribe's artists to run, where they can sell their own work."

"That's really impressive. I didn't realize the reservation boundaries were so close. I mean, I knew they were nearby, but I didn't realize…" Her words trailed off as she went back into the house for a moment to drop off the last of the dishes.

When she returned, Tom watched her to see what she would do. Much to his relief, she poured more wine for them both and moved over to the padded bench that faced the water at the far end of the patio. Tom joined her there, sitting next to her as they sipped their wine and watched the dark waves rippling in the moonlight. The dim light from the patio behind them didn't interfere with the stillness of the night all around them.

Tom reached over and put his arm around her, gratified when she moved closer, snuggling into his side. They sat there for a while, watching the stars twinkle and the water wash against the sandy shore. It was a peaceful night, the sound of the water soothing, even while the feel of Ashley against him heated his blood.

CHAPTER EIGHT

Ashley was about to scream in frustration. If Tom didn't make a move in the next five seconds, she was going to jump him.

Oh, to hell with five seconds!

Ashley got up and rearranged herself so that she straddled Tom's thighs, her hands sliding around his neck as she lowered her mouth to his. And then, she was kissing him. Thank God.

She couldn't have taken one more quiet moment without jumping his delectably handsome bones. Tom's only fault—if it really could be called a fault—was that he was too polite. Any other guy would have been all over her by now, but something was holding Tom back. He seemed a little nervous, maybe even a little shy, but Ashley didn't mind showing him that she was ready. More than ready. She had been going a little nuts just sitting there, next to him, feeling his warmth, and breathing in his enticing scent.

Things were better now. She could taste him and feel him under her. She liked the way his cock stood to attention as she introduced her thighs to his, rubbing all over as she squirmed on his lap. Tom's arms went around her waist, supporting her, then subtly moving her in the direction he wanted her to go…right against his hard cock.

She could feel him through the layers of clothing, and he was…impressive. Oh, yeah. Impressive was definitely the word for him.

Her head swam when he whirled with her in his arms, changing positions as he put her beneath him on the wide, padded bench. He was so damn strong. It was a total turn on. He lifted her as if she weighed nothing at all. She felt petite next to him, which wasn't something she normally felt with guys. She was the tallest of her sisters, and though none of them were waif-thin, she was built a little more…uh…substantially than her sisters.

Her height and curves had made her feel self-conscious with a lot of guys, but it seemed none of those old insecurities plagued her when she was with Tom. He was a big man. Taller than she was, his body was coated in hard, rippling muscles. He treated her like she was a goddess, and with him, she felt it. Just a little.

Make that a lot.

He undressed her, moving faster now that he knew she was eager for more. She urged him on, helping by tugging at his clothes, undoing the small buttons on his shirt and his dress pants. He dressed very urbanely for a bear, she thought, smiling.

And she'd give anything, right about now, to see him in nothing at all.

Apparently, that's what he wanted too because he didn't stop stripping her, even while he was kissing the breath from her body. He let her up for air, only to begin a new assault as his mouth trailed hot, wet kisses down over her skin, pausing at all the interesting places.

He laved her nipples with his tongue, making her moan. He nibbled his way down her ribcage and over her tummy. And then, he was there, between her splayed thighs, his mouth giving her the most intimate kiss imaginable while his hands roamed over her thighs, caressing and squeezing, holding them far apart for his pleasure.

She felt mastered and cherished, all at the same time. Never before had she felt this way with a man. Tom knew what he wanted, and he made it exactly what she wanted too. Anything. She'd give him anything by the time she came apart under the powerful influence of his tongue on her clit and up her channel. He knew just how to play her to make her scream.

And scream she did. His name echoed through the trees around the patio a split second before he rose up and slid into her quaking body. He held her thighs high and wide while he took possession of her spasming channel, his gaze holding hers while her orgasm went on and on...to heights she'd never visited before.

He began to move, and she kept climaxing in the most intense experience of her life.

Multiple orgasms. She thought maybe that's what they called this. Wasn't it supposed to be some kind of unattainable phenomena?

If so, nobody had told Tom. He rode her hard and kept the sensations running hot as he escalated quickly into his own raging climax. When he stiffened above her and she felt him come, tears leaked out of her eyes at the beauty of the moment…and the man.

He'd given her something she had never had before. He'd made her feel…almost…loved.

Tom wanted roar as he came inside her, but he did his best to leash the bear's howl of triumph. Everything inside him shouted *mate*, but though he inwardly crowed, he knew he'd have to take it slowly with Ashley. The last thing he wanted to do was scare her off.

He wouldn't talk about mating until she had seen Brody and Nell's relationship at work for a while, he decided. She needed to understand that mating was for life, and that he'd never treat her badly. He would live only for her, but he had to finesse her agreement. He had to show her that he was serious, and that the mating impulse, though quick to make itself known, wasn't capricious in any way.

Tom rolled to his back on the wide base of the padded bench and draped Ashley over him as they both came down from a glorious climax. She fit him perfectly, as he had hoped she would. She was his match in every way, and he would spend the rest of his life proving himself worthy of her.

If she let him.

When the night air started to cool, Tom knew it was time to go indoors. Would she stay? There was only one way to find out.

"Shall we move this party to where it's warmer?" he asked, hoping with every fiber of his being that she'd say yes.

Ashley leaned up, her hair tumbling around them, creating an intimate space in which their gazes met and held. She smiled, rubbing one finger along his collarbone.

"I thought you'd never ask."

She made a move to get up, but he stopped her, taking her easily into his arms and rising from the bench. Kicking the wad of clothes toward the patio door, he set her down right in front so he could open the door without fear of dropping her.

Ashley scooped up the pile of their discarded clothing, though he would've left it, and scampered into the house before he could stop her. He followed her in, finding her sorting and folding their clothes on the kitchen counter. She was a neat little thing, which amused him.

But there would be time for clothes

folding later. Much later.

Tom scooped her into his arms and carried her straight down the long hall to his bedroom.

* * *

Sometime well before dawn, Tom came awake. Ashley was moving quietly around the bedroom.

"What's up?" he asked, yawning as he scratched his chest.

"Me, unfortunately," came Ashley's swift reply. "Sorry to wake you, but I really have to go."

"Go?" Maybe he hadn't heard her correctly.

"Yeah. I've got to open the bakery. Actually, I'm already late." She ducked into the bathroom while he got out of bed.

Dammit. He had heard her correctly. After the most glorious night of his life, his new lover had to leave.

But he understood. Her family was depending on her to take the first shift, as she always did. They hadn't made any prior arrangements that would allow someone to cover for her. Events had just unfolded the night before. There hadn't been a whole lot of planning or premeditation.

Frankly, Tom hadn't expected anything beyond dinner when he issued his invitation. He'd hoped. But hope wasn't the same thing as certainty. The fact that Ashley had spent the night in his arms was something he would never regret. It was a special gift. A blessing.

And he would do everything in his power to keep her. Forever.

Part of that kind of relationship, he knew, involved allowing the other person room to grow, and be who they were without interference. It was accepting them as they were, and not trying to change them to suit his needs.

Ashley was a baker. She was a vital part of her family's business. She worked while most other people slept. It was her routine.

Tom wasn't going to interfere with that. Not on what was, essentially, their second date. It would be up to Ashley, if she wanted to change her schedule, now that they were a couple.

She probably didn't realize it yet, but in Tom's mind, being a couple was a foregone conclusion. He just had to ease her into the idea. Eventually, though, she would see them as he did—two halves of a whole.

Ashley came out of the bathroom, a towel wrapped around her and a fragrant cloud of steam following on her heels. She'd used his soap and shampoo. His bear scented the familiar fragrances, plus the essence of Ashley that made those plain scents much more alluring. Tom liked that she would wear his scents—his soaps and his touch—all day.

"I hope you don't mind. I won't have time to clean up when I get back to the bakery. The bread has to go in the oven as soon as I can prepare it, or I'll have a few angry patrons in a couple of hours."

"No problem," Tom said, gently reassuring her. He wanted to be supportive, even if he would rather have slept until morning, with her in his arms. "I'll drive you back."

Tom ducked into the bathroom, pausing only to place a smacking kiss on her lips as he passed her. He saw her head out of the bedroom and figured she was going after her clothes.

He grabbed some clean clothes out of his wardrobe a few minutes later, dressing quickly. Venturing out in search of Ashley, he found her in his kitchen, fully dressed, if a little rumpled. She looked nervous, and he hated the uncertainty that marred her pretty face.

"I'm sorry," she said, as he came into the room. "I know this is a strange way to end the evening."

"Don't worry." Tom walked up to her and took her into his arms, rocking her gently. "I didn't exactly plan last night either, but I'm really glad it happened. I want to spend more time with you, Ashley. And I don't mind if I have to do a little readjusting of my schedule to make it work. I'm mostly an artist, these days. I don't have to be anywhere at a particular time, most days. And my legal work is mostly paperwork, which can be done in the middle of the night, if need be. I've got more flexibility in my hours than you do. We'll figure something out." He kissed her, then moved back to meet her gaze. "That is…if you want to continue exploring this thing between us. I know I do." He smiled at her, hoping she'd give him the answer he really wanted. "How about it, Ash? What do you say?"

"I say…yes." She reached up to kiss him quickly, smiling brightly. "I want to see where this leads, but right now, it better lead me to the bakery pretty soon, or the morning's bread will never get made." She stepped out of his arms, and he felt momentarily bereft. He craved the feel of her in his embrace already.

But she hadn't told him to get lost. That was a plus. He could work with it. He just had to be cautious and not rush her.

CHAPTER NINE

Ashley had expected Tom to just drop her off. Instead, he'd come into the bakery with her, keeping her company as she rushed through making the day's bread. He was a good companion. He didn't get in the way, and his conversation was both interesting and subdued, befitting the early hour.

When she had the first batch in the oven, they took a break together. He'd made the coffee and poured her a cup when she came out from behind the oven door, ushering her to one of the tables, where they could look out at the view. They sipped the hot liquid in companionable silence for a few minutes as the sun's first faint rays began to make an appearance.

"If I didn't say so before, I had a lovely time last night," Ashley finally opened the topic she'd been avoiding for the past hour.

When it came down to it, she was actually somewhat shy, even if she had jumped Tom's bones a few hours ago.

"So did I," he agreed amiably. "Want to do it again tonight? I can get some fresh fish from Sig, if you like grilled salmon."

She felt a smile bloom inside her soul. "I'd like that."

"I'll come by and pick you up again?" he asked, though it wasn't really a question.

"Sounds good." She grinned. Just like that, she had another date with him. Another chance to prove to him that they were good together. No. Not just *good*. Spectacular.

Tom stayed for breakfast, sharing what was fast becoming a ritual with them, of feeding Gus the seagull and sitting outside for a bit, watching the sun rise. When the first customers started trickling in, Tom sat quietly at one of the out-of-the-way tables, reading email on his cell phone while he ate a Danish and drank coffee.

Everyone greeted him in some way, either nodding or going over to shake hands, and she got the idea that a great deal of speculation was flying as they looked from him to her and back again. Ashley didn't know what to make of it. For her part, she didn't mind anybody knowing that she was dating Tom, but she didn't really know how he felt about their possible notoriety. It was a very small town, after all.

She watched him carefully as each new person said hello, but he didn't seem to care that the other townsfolk were putting two and two together and coming up with four. Maybe he didn't mind that they knew. Or maybe—and this sort of speculation could get her in trouble—just maybe, he *wanted* them to know that he and Ash were an item.

Maybe his very obvious presence in the bakery this morning was meant to stake some sort of claim, or warn other men off. A little thrill of excitement sizzled down her spine at the thought, but she had to be careful. She could be totally misreading the situation. Maybe he just wanted to hang out, drink coffee, and eat pastries. It wasn't all that uncommon.

Although…up 'til a couple of days ago, Tom hadn't even set foot in the store before. And now, it seemed he couldn't get enough of the place. At least in the morning, when she was there.

Nell showed up mid-morning. Brody

dropped her off and stopped by the table Tom had claimed to chat. Tom wasn't sure he wanted to talk about anything serious just yet, but if anyone would understand how he felt about Ashley, Brody would be the man.

"How's it going?" Brody asked casually, taking one of the empty seats at the small table. He placed his cup of coffee on the table and bit into a honey bun he held in his other hand.

"It's going really well, I think," Tom said, his gaze following Ashley as she moved behind the counter.

"You got it bad, bro," Brody commented after a short interlude where he devoured the rest of the pastry while Tom sipped coffee and watched Ashley.

Tom put down the coffee cup and looked at his friend. "Yeah, I do," he admitted. "You got any advice for me?"

"Don't fuck it up," Brody answered immediately, capping off his words of wisdom with a shit-eating grin.

"Perhaps I should have said, do you have any advice besides the obvious?" Tom clarified. They'd been friends for a long time, and he was used to the kind of banter Brody enjoyed.

"Treat her right," Brody added, pausing to think. "Don't rush her." He sipped his coffee. "And make her happy." He placed the empty coffee cup on the table. "Do those three little things, and you should be okay."

"What's it like, mating a human?" Tom felt the need to ask. He knew it was more common for bears to mate with humans than most other shifters, but none of their immediate friends had mated until Brody found Nell.

"She's more fragile than a shifter woman," Brody answered honestly. "But my Nell has a core of steel. She's stronger than she looks—both emotionally and physically. I'm afraid sometimes, that my strength and size is too much for her, but she promised to let me know when I go too far. As of this morning, she's only had to do that once."

Tom frowned. What had Brody done that his mate objected to?

"She doesn't like the teeth every time," Brody explained without Tom needing to ask. He pointed to his own neck. "She said she's proud to wear my marks, but not every single day. And she did have a good point about not knowing who might wander into the bakery. She can't pass in the human world with bite marks on her neck very well, and this town is open for visitors, even if we still control who stays."

"Wise decision," Tom agreed, seeing the logic of Nell not wanting to wear visible bite marks that would raise questions if humans saw them.

Brody stood, collecting his trash. "Are you going to John's for the planning meeting?"

"Yeah, I was just about to head over there." Tom stood also, noting the way the business in the bakery had picked up in the past few minutes. "I'll go with you," he told Brody, since they were headed in the same direction.

Not wanting to interrupt Ashley's work, he waved to her as he walked toward the door with Brody. Ashley smiled and waved back, even as she waited on a customer. Tom went out the door with a feeling of joy in his heart. She had put it there. Ashley. His mate.

CHAPTER TEN

The planning meeting was something they held every week. It usually started just before noon and went on most of the afternoon. Tom's date with Ashley wasn't until later. He calculated he'd have just enough time to drop by the fish market and pick up the salmon from Sig before picking her up.

They discussed the applications for business permits that had come in over the past few weeks and the plans for further construction John had initiated. They were going to do most of the building themselves, but for the new town hall, John had sought proposals from two different construction companies, both shifter-owned.

They discussed the two approaches, and Tom wasn't surprised when the better design proved to have come from Redstone

Construction. Those werecougars had a top-notch operation and a well-earned reputation. If it was solely up to Tom, he'd give them the contract and be done with it, but John liked to think his little town was something of a democracy with a benevolent Alpha running the whole thing. He was putting it up for a vote next week after the two plans had been discussed and dissected to his satisfaction.

They were winding down the meeting when Brody's radio squawked.

"Sheriff, there's a situation at the bakery," came Zak Flambeau's disembodied voice over the walkie-talkie.

Tom stiffened. Ashley was probably off-shift at this time of day, but it was still her family's business, and her sisters were there. If there was a problem, Tom needed to know what it was, so he could help.

Brody looked upset as he keyed the mic on the radio. "Sitrep," he ordered, falling back on their military training.

"A reporter was just in, asking a whole lot of questions. Nell called the station, looking for you, but when I told her you were in a meeting, she hung up. I ran over to the bakery to find out what was going on, and now, I'm calling you."

Tom knew that when Zak said he'd *run* over, he meant it literally. The sheriff's office was only a few doors down from the bakery on Main Street.

"Good man," Brody commented. "Stay there and keep watch. I'm coming."

Tom stood as Brody nodded at John. "I'm going too," he said to the room at large, nodding as well to the Alpha.

"Is there something I should know?" John asked, some of the Alpha tone of command entering his voice.

"Yes," Tom answered without hesitation. "But it's complicated. And it's not really my secret to tell, though I don't think the ladies will mind now that they know about us. But I will tell you this—Ashley Baker doesn't know it yet, but she's my mate."

Tom saw the varied reactions of his closest friends. To a man, they all looked happy for him, and several undoubtedly would have jumped up to congratulate him if he wasn't on his way out the door. As it was, they were all smiling and most nodded to him, acknowledging the claim.

That was significant. He'd let them know that Ashley was his. By acknowledging his claim, they were saying that they wouldn't interfere. In fact, these men—the closest he had to brothers in the world—would probably do all they could to help him along in his pursuit of the lady.

"Understood," John said, nodding. "And congratulations." He didn't smile. The Alpha was probably more concerned about what the women—and Tom—could have been hiding. "I'll be right behind you. Expect me in a few minutes. I'll want an explanation as to why you didn't give me the full briefing before we invited them into our midst," John said with a bit of menace in his tone as Brody and Tom headed for the door.

Tom didn't regret exercising his judgment on what to tell John and everyone else when he'd been tasked to investigate the Baker sisters' backgrounds. But he knew he would have to do some fast talking when John arrived. Tom wasn't worried about it, but he knew John could growl with the best of them, and he wouldn't let John's intimidation tactics frighten the ladies.

Brody and Tom stormed the bakery a few minutes later, much as they had once stormed enemy strongholds together in far off lands. Only this was friendly territory, and nothing more sinister than a few loaves of bread awaited them inside.

Brody's deputy, Zak, was waiting for them in the seating area. He came forward to meet them at the door when Brody and Tom walked in. Tom kept going, leaving Zak to give Brody the sitrep, while he went to check on the women. At this hour of the day, it was the overlap period between the end of Nell's shift and the beginning of Tina's.

Nell was up front with Brody, having gone straight to him as soon as he walked in. That left the youngest sister, Tina, in back behind the counter.

"Are you okay?" Tom asked, coming right around the counter and checking things over to satisfy himself that everything was secure in the back. "Where's Ashley?"

"I'm spitting mad, but okay. Ash is upstairs, hiding," she answered succinctly.

Seeing that Tina was all right, Tom had to get to Ashley. He pushed through to the stairs that led up to the sisters' apartment and took them two at a time. Ashley pulled open the door at the top as he neared it, and when he cleared the threshold, she launched herself into his arms.

He held her, feeling her body tremble

with fear. He didn't like the sensation, and he vowed again to protect her from anything that could possibly harm her.

"Ssh, honey. It'll be all right." He tried to soothe her, but she was going from scared to angry and back again. He could feel the fluctuations in her temper as he held her securely in his arms.

"How can you say that?" she demanded angrily. "A *reporter* found me! The bastard was bothering my sisters, asking about me, asking when I'd be working the counter. Threatening that he'd stake out the place until he found me and got his scoop." She was crying nervous tears by the end of her angry speech, but Tom held her, rocking her back and forth.

"We can handle one little reporter, sweetheart. The entire Clan is behind you. They won't let anything happen here. More than that, *I* won't let anything happen. I'll tear the reporter apart with my bare hands before I let him reveal your location to anyone."

But she wasn't really listening. "I'll have to move again," she whispered brokenly.

Tom set her away from him and made her meet his gaze. "Stop right there, Ashley.

You're not going anywhere. You're happy here in Grizzly Cove, aren't you?"

She seemed to come to her senses. "Happier than I've been in a long time," she admitted, her gaze still holding echoes of defeat.

"That's good to hear because you've made me happier than I've been in a long time too. I'm not willing to give that up so easily. Are you?" he challenged.

She shook her head, but her expression looked agonized. "I just don't see how this can possibly work out. I've been found. He'll tell others, and then, we'll have no peace here whatsoever. For your people's protection, I'll have to leave and take my troubles with me."

"Honey, you're one of us now. You're part of our community. We're not going to let anything bad happen."

"You keep saying that, but I just don't see how." She shook her head, her expression pitiful.

"For starters, we're circling the wagons. Brody and Zak are downstairs, and Big John is on his way here. We're going to have to tell him about you, so he understands what he's up against. He's not going to be happy,

99

and he'll probably growl a bit, but don't worry. He's a good guy under the Alpha bluster. He'll do the right thing."

She cringed, but she was listening. "And then what?"

"Then I believe I'm going to have a little chat with the reporter." Tom was looking forward to it. He'd kill the man if he refused to leave. Nothing was off limits when it came to protecting his mate.

"No, Tom! You can't. It'll only be worse if you try to scare him off. He'll know for sure then that I'm here. Right now, he's still wondering. He doesn't know for sure. We need to keep it that way as long as we can."

Tom considered her point. "Okay. So maybe *chat* was the wrong word. What if our reporter friend found himself confronted by a bear? Or two? Or maybe a whole bunch of us?" Tom started to grin, imagining the fun of running the reporter out of town on a rail without ever speaking a word.

"That actually sounds like a really good idea," came John's voice from behind Tom's back.

Tom had heard the Alpha's deliberately heavy tread on the stairs and wasn't surprised by his presence. Nell and Brody were right behind him, and they all trooped past Ashely and Tom into the apartment, moving into the living room.

Ashley stepped back from Tom, leaving his embrace and wiping at her eyes. She seemed to be in a state of mild shock, her gaze following the small crowd that had just invaded her home. She walked toward the living room, but Tom caught her hand.

"We do this together, Ash," he whispered. "Remember, John's growl is worse than his bite."

"I heard that," John groused from the living room.

"Damn shifter hearing," Tom joked for Ashley's sake.

Together, they walked into the living room, hand in hand.

CHAPTER ELEVEN

Tom wasn't exactly happy to have to explain about Ashley's problem to John, but though the Alpha growled a bit—as predicted—it wasn't really that bad. In fact, as soon as John became aware of the full extent of the situation, he was as supportive of Ashley as Tom could have hoped.

"So what can we do to deter this reporter from asking any more questions?" Brody asked once the facts had been fully explained. "If it was the old west, we could run him out of town on a rail, tarred and feathered, but somehow, I don't think that would go over too well in this day and age."

"I liked Tom's idea," John said. "We could go bear on his ass and scare him off. Where's the guy staying?"

"Zak discovered he was camping on National Park land, not too far away," Brody supplied as John grinned.

"That's just about perfect," John said, looking a lot like the cat who swallowed the canary, no matter that he was a big assed grizzly shifter.

* * *

Ashley sat with her sisters, waiting for word of the men. Brody, Tom, Big John and a few of the others had gone off in search of the reporter's campsite a few hours ago. The bakery was long since closed, but the girls couldn't rest until the guys were back safe and they knew what had happened up in the woods.

"Do you think they'll be okay?" Nell asked for the twentieth time, pacing and hugging herself as she worried.

Nobody answered. Nobody *had* an answer. The sisters were handling their worry in different ways. Nell was pacing. Ash was curled up on the couch, hugging a pillow. Tina was by the window, looking out on the quiet street.

Nothing much happened in town at this late hour. The occasional bear might stroll through the woods or down by the water, but they mostly kept well out of sight. Tonight, though, there was a more visible presence as Zak sat in the deputy's SUV, just down the street, on a stakeout. He'd been stationed there, Brody had told Nell, to make sure the town stayed as quiet as it should be while the other guys held their surprise party in the woods.

They'd been gone for a few hours when Tina finally broke her silent vigil. "I see Brody's truck coming down the street," she said, her voice full of intensity.

Ashley jumped off the couch and threw the pillow aside. She stopped before she hit the window, not wanting to be visible just in case the reporter or any of his friends were watching from below. Nell had no such compunction and went right up to the window and looked out on the street.

"What's going on?" Ashley asked from behind her sisters.

"The truck is stopping," Nell reported. "Brody's getting out," she said, then turned quickly. "I'm going down to let them in."

But Ashley was already on her way to the stairs, heading down into the bakery at a fast clip. She halted at the bottom, allowing Nell and Tina to go ahead of her, for the same reasons she'd stayed away from the window. Until she heard how the guys' little raid had gone, she wouldn't take anything for granted.

Nell raced ahead to open the door for Brody. He hugged her as he walked in the door, sweeping her in with him as he stood aside to let the other guys enter. Much to Ashley's relief, Tom was right behind him, laughing at something John said as he brought up the rear.

The men were grinning from ear to ear, laughing like schoolboys, at times, and Ashley felt relief in her heart to see them all safe—especially Tom. She walked forward to meet him and was thrilled when he reached out and swept her into his arms, twirling her around the room for a breathless moment.

When he put her down, he gave her smacking kiss as his enthusiasm spilled over, making her laugh. Whatever had happened, it had left the men in an ebullient mood.

"Ash, you should've been there," Tom enthused. "We had that city slicker crapping his pants and crying for his mama before we let him escape." He made little quotation marks in the air as he said that final word. "He jumped in his car so fast he left behind most of his gear."

"We now know his home address, his name and social security number," John confirmed, flipping through a brown leather wallet that had to be the reporter's. "With that, we can wreak havoc on him, the likes of which he can't even imagine." John's laugh was slightly evil, but in a loveable sort of way.

"You wouldn't do that, would you?" Ashley had to ask.

John seemed to consider. "If he comes back, we can take this one step at a time, but if he insists on screwing with us, I won't hesitate to do all in my power to fuck him up in every way possible." John's tone of voice was as serious as Ashley had ever heard it.

"And when Big John says the reporter is screwing with *us*, he means all of us, honey. You, me, your sisters. We're all family. Clan. We protect each other." Tom's arms came around her from behind, hugging her. "Believe me now?" he asked in a rumble right next to her ear.

She turned around in his embrace, pulling him close. She couldn't speak for a moment, overcome by emotion. When she had a bit of control again, she turned to face the others.

"I can't thank you enough for this," she said finally.

"No problem, sweetheart," John answered, his smile returning. "I haven't had this much fun in a long time. You should've seen that guy run." John and the others dissolved into guffaws and laughing comments about the way the reporter had screamed and scampered away when confronted by a half dozen big, angry bears.

"I don't know what he made of the polar bear," Brody mumbled, setting the men off laughing again. "I didn't expect Sven to come on the raid, but it was good to have him along. Confused the hell out of that reporter."

"Maybe he thought he was seeing a ghost. All that white fur in the pitch black forest," John added, chuckling.

As the laughter died down again, Ashley turned to hug Tom. "I was so worried the guy might've had a gun. I know you're fierce and all, but what if he'd shot you?"

"Oh, honey," Tom crooned to her, stroking her hair. "It takes more than one or two conventional bullets to stop one of us. And we're all ex-military. We've faced guns before. Many times. We know what we're doing. Even if he had been armed, he wouldn't have been given a chance to get even one shot off at any of us."

"As it is, we confiscated his weapons as well as his personal belongings," Brody put in.

Ashley whirled to face the deputy who was now part of the family. "He *was* armed?"

"*Was* being the operational word there, Ash," Brody reminded her. "When he saw us bearing down on him, he ran. The little arsenal he had in his tent was useless to him, but it'll provide further ammunition—if you'll pardon the pun—against him. Most of those firearms aren't quite legal for him to be carrying here. I've got them locked up in the back of my truck, and he's not getting them back."

Ashley couldn't believe how casually they were all taking this news, but then again, they were vets. Maybe weapons weren't that big a deal to them, like they were to civilians.

"Regardless, I'm glad you guys are whole, and I'm really incredibly touched that you'd help me this way. Thank you from the bottom of my heart." Words were inadequate to express the wealth of feeling, but they would have to suffice for now.

She'd find a way to thank everyone for standing by her. Somehow. Someday. She'd return the favor, with interest.

"Think nothing of it, Ashley. Welcome to the community and just know that you are under the protection of our Clan, such as it is. You may not be a bear, but you have the heart of one," John said, looking from Ash to Tom and back again. "I'm out of here. Gotta get some sleep to be properly mayoral tomorrow. I'm hoping the reporter will call." He grinned as he walked out, leaving the two couples and Tina.

Tina was the next to leave. "I'm going upstairs. I'm glad everybody is okay." She yawned as she headed for the stairs, leaving the two couples behind.

"We're outta here too," Brody said next, ushering Nell toward the door. His truck was still parked at the curb. "See you guys tomorrow."

"Thanks, Brody," Ashley called after them. "See ya tomorrow, sis."

"At last, we're alone," Tom mused as the door shut behind the other couple.

Ashley laughed, despite the worry that had come before. "I'm so glad you're okay," she said, running her fingers through his hair. "I was so worried."

CHAPTER TWELVE

"Wanna go to my place?" Tom asked, but Ashley shook her head.

"I don't want to leave Tina here alone, just in case that reporter comes back." Tom looked resigned, but he nodded. He seemed about to pull away from her when she placed one hand on his shoulder. "But my room has a queen size bed, and the walls are pretty thick. Why don't you come upstairs?"

Tom grinned, and it was as if the sun had come out in her soul. "I thought you'd never ask."

Ashley paused to lock up, Tom at her side. When all was secure, they went up the stairs together, eager steps taking them quickly through the apartment to her room, which was at the front of the building. She had one of the two bedrooms that had the great view of the cove.

Nell had claimed the other front room but had been spending most of her nights at Brody's since they'd gotten engaged. Poor Tina had been stuck with the bedroom at the back of the building, but that worked in Ashley's favor now, since it was doubtful Tina would hear anything, even if Tom made Ashley scream with pleasure. Which, after last night, she realized, was a very real possibility.

But Tom didn't pounce on her the moment the door was shut. Instead, he sat with her on the edge of the bed, taking her hands in his. The moment felt serious, and Ashley frowned, feeling doubt creep in. Was he going to ask to slow things down? Was he going to dump her?

"Ashley," Tom began, his tone so serious she began to fret. "There are a few things I want to discuss with you."

He seemed to be waiting for her to respond. "Yes?" She was proud that her voice sounded much steadier than her nerves.

"I hope you know by now that I will protect you to my dying breath."

Whoa. Heavy. But was there a silent *but* on the end of that amazing sentence? When he didn't continue right away, she felt the need to make another response. Was he waiting for her to acknowledge every sentence, or maybe… Was he nervous too? Her fears started to recede a little.

"I hope it never comes to that," she said with a nervous laugh. "But I'm grateful that you feel so protective of me. I can use all the help I can get with my past coming back to haunt me like this."

"Honey, you'll never have to worry about that again, as far as I'm concerned. In fact…" He paused, turning a little more toward her, rubbing his thumbs over her knuckles as he held her hands in his. "I don't want to rush this, but, Ash, you should know that when a shifter meets his mate, he often knows almost right away. Like how quickly Brody and your sister got together. That was pretty quick, right?"

"Yeah, sort of a whirlwind romance, you might say," she agreed, wondering where he was going with this. Could he possibly mean…?

"Well, that's normal for us. Some species know on first scenting their mate. Some— the big cats—know they've met their mate when they purr in human form, which is something only their true mate can bring about. We believe that the Mother of All has a hand in helping us find that one special person meant just for us. Ashley..." he moved closer to her, his voice very serious, "...I knew last night, when we made love, that you are my mate. I want to be with you for the rest of our lives, and your happiness and safety is at the center of my world."

Ashley was speechless for a moment as an incredulous sort of joy filled her being.

"Really?" She could hardly believe what he was saying. This wasn't a whirlwind romance. This was a tornado. A benevolent but still shocking tornado. "You know that fast?"

"I do," he answered solemnly. "But the question is, can you return my feelings? Will you be my mate? My wife, in human terms, though you should know, mating is forever. There will never be another woman for me. Just you, Ashley Baker, 'til the day I leave this world. And even then, I'll await you on the other side, until we can be together again. I love you. And I will always love you."

Ashley felt tears gathering behind her eyes. They spilled down her cheeks at his profession of love. It was the most beautiful thing any man had ever said to her, made all the more poignant because it was Tom who was saying such wonderful things.

She launched herself into his arms, talking next to his ear, though her words were garbled with happy tears.

"I love you too, Tom. So much. I can't imagine how this happened so fast, but I can't imagine my life without you in it." She kissed him, little kisses wherever she could reach—the side of his face, his ear, his neck. "Yes," she whispered, her heart in her throat. "Yes, I'll be your mate. I don't want anyone else. After you, I could never be with anybody else. You're it for me, mister."

He moved her head so he could claim her lips, cradling her face in his warm, strong palms.

They wound up on the bed long minutes later, having undressed each other with careless abandon. Ashley had taken charge, coming down over Tom while he smiled up at her, his hands on her hips, guiding her motion as she rode him. She liked the feeling of power, the hard ridges of his muscles under her thighs and against her palms.

Tom liked it too. She could see the

indulgent smile and lazy enjoyment in his half-lidded eyes. He was such a handsome man, in every way. When he'd been tough, ready to take on the world earlier this evening before he went out with the other guys, she had seen the warrior side of his personality. Now she was seeing the lover, once again. She liked everything she'd seen of him and still couldn't quite believe she'd get to watch him grow old with her for the rest of their lives. She would enjoy learning everything about him—especially how best to please him.

She tried different rhythms, different motions, until she found one that he seemed to particularly enjoy. She rode him hard and kept increasing the pace until, at the last, he had to guide her hips as she lost control. She spasmed around him, and he came soon after, jerking his body upward, sealing them together for long moments as he came deep within her.

They lazed in the aftermath, before round two, side by side in her bed. It was just barely big enough for both of them, but neither one was complaining. Ashley drew little patterns on his chest with one finger as she lay on her side, his arm tucked around her.

"You know, after you marry me, you could practice law again, if you want. I could use some help. I get a little too adversarial, sometimes, when a tenacious human lawyer gets combative. You could run interference so I don't accidentally, on purpose, rip some jerk's head off." He chuckled as she stilled. "Plus, you're a great lawyer. Nothing that happened to you was your fault. And when you marry me, you can take my last name and begin again with a new identity. Nobody needs to know about your past. You'd be a great help to the town as it grows, and to the Clan. It'd be a shame to let all your education and hard work go to waste. That is, if you want to. No pressure. You can do whatever you like. I'm just offering up the possibility."

"I hadn't even considered every practicing again, but you're right. I went to law school because I really wanted to help people. I've enjoyed the bakery, but that was my sisters' dream. Not mine. Not really. I've liked helping them, but I would like to at least look into the idea of reclaiming my profession, if you really think it's possible." She reached up to kiss him. "You're amazing for even thinking of it. I love you, Tom. You're a heck of a great guy."

He grinned at her. "I love you too, my mate. I never thought I'd find you, and you've been here for months. I should've come into the bakery a lot sooner. I'm sorry it took me so long to get here."

"All that matters is that you're here now, and I'm not ever letting you go."

"Amen to that."

# # #

EXCERPT:
NIGHT SHIFT
Grizzly Cove #3

CHAPTER ONE

Zak really liked the new duty Sheriff Brody Chambers had him working. Every night since a reporter had come to town to try to make trouble for Ashley, the middle of the three Baker sisters, the sheriff, who was now mated to the eldest sister, Nell, had sent Zak to watch over the youngest sister, Tina. Tina worked the night shift at the bakery the three sisters owned, and since it was the only place that served food in their new town so far, a lot of people frequented it.

The baked goods were downright delicious. The sisters used natural ingredients, including a lot of honey, which was a favorite of Zak's and most of the town, for that matter. It was true that bears really did like the sweet stuff.

Zak had been admiring Tina from afar since she'd moved to town, but hadn't really had much chance to get close to her since they both worked the night shift. He hadn't had much reason to stop in at the bakery while on duty until now, and he was taking full advantage of the sheriff's request that he keep an eye on the one remaining, unmated sister.

Brody had claimed the eldest sister, and about two weeks later, Tom Masdan, the town lawyer had announced his relationship with the middle sister, Ashley. Turns out, they were both lawyers, though Ashley had given up a high-powered career when a rat in her New York firm had made her look bad and inadvertently caused grief for her client. Unfortunately the client had been very high profile and tragedy had resulted from the poorly handled court case. Ashley had needed to go into hiding from the press, which she had, right here in Grizzly Cove, working at her sisters' bakery.

In this tiny town, there were only two lawmen at the moment. Brody worked days and Zak overlapped in the afternoon, then worked the evenings alone, unless there was trouble. Both of them were always on call, but then again, since all of the men who formed the nucleus of the new community had served together in the military, just about everyone in town could act as backup, if needed. It was just that Brody and Zak had been handed the roles of sheriff and deputy when the Alpha, Big John, had been assigning tasks according to each man's abilities and desires.

They'd all retired from the military now, though none of them were old by human standards. They were, to a man, bear shifters of one kind or another. The majority, including the Alpha, were grizzlies, but there was at least one polar bear, a couple of Kodiaks, a big-assed Russian bear and a few black bears. Zak Flambeau was one of the latter. Smaller than his grizzly friends, Zak was no less deadly. And though he'd taken his share of guff from his buddies over the years, he knew they respected his skills as a marksman and as a shifter. He was smaller, but that also meant he was a lot quicker and more agile than some of his larger buddies. He'd used that to his advantage many times in the field. But now all that was over. He was retired from that life. It was a bit of an adjustment.

Big John had come up with the insane idea to build their own town from scratch. He'd been quietly buying up land over the years and when the time came, he'd laid out his idea for the rest of his men. They'd balked a bit at first. After all, Big John wanted them masquerade as an artists' colony, for cripes sake. They weren't artists. Although, most of the guys had given it the old college try and come up with some passable *objet d'art*, Zak had to admit.

He couldn't draw his way out of a paper bag. He couldn't even do self-portraits of his bear half, using a chainsaw and a stump of wood. He left that to Brody. Zak didn't have a talent like that. Nothing in the visual arts, anyway. If he had any talent at all, he'd have said it was for cooking, but he couldn't see a way to turn his Cajun heritage of spicy, down home dishes into an art form that could contribute to the town's artists' colony status.

So he contented himself with being the deputy. Good ol' Barney Pfife to Brody's Andy Taylor. That he could handle. Blindfolded. And with one hand tied behind his back.

Running security was second nature to him. Zak had left home at eighteen, leaving the bayou and his bastard father behind, striking out to join the Army. He'd never looked back. Not even once.

When his mate had died of illness, Zak's father had turned mean. Or maybe he'd always been mean, and losing his mate just made him worse. Zak didn't know for sure. His mother had died when he was still a boy. He missed her to this very day, but he felt like maybe sometimes she was watching over him from above—or wherever spirits went when they left this realm.

"You know, deputy, I'm going to have to start charging you rent if you keep coming in here every night." Tina brought over the carafe of coffee, pouring him a fresh cup without even asking. She knew by now that he would never say no to good coffee.

"Just following orders, ma'am. Though to be honest, I'm enjoying these orders way more than any other I've been given to date in this town. It's nice to have an excuse to sit here, drink coffee and eat your marvelous pastries." He popped a slice of the danish he'd been eating into his mouth to emphasize his point.

"But you ran the reporter off. Nobody's seen him since. I don't think he's coming back, and even if he did, I could handle him. I'd tell him to go straight to hell, like I did the first time he came sniffing around."

Tina was a little more outspoken than her older sisters, and Zak liked that about her. She had spirit. But that sort of spirit could sometimes get a person into trouble.

"I won't argue the point, but Brody asked me to keep an eye on the place and I'm just as happy to do so. Come on, *ma chere*, don't tell me you don't enjoy my company, at least a little."

The little bell above the door tinkled out its merry tune as the door opened, and every hackle on Zak's body rose in alarm. He spun to face the newcomer, taking in the dark, wet clothing, the blood-red eyes and the hesitant gait.

"Holy shit." Zak grabbed for his radio as the newcomer eyed him.

"Call your Alpha little cub. I am hanging on here by a thread."

Zak's sensitive nose smelled the blood— new and old—on the creature in the doorway. That he was probably outgunned and outclassed entered his mind briefly, but he dismissed the idea. All that mattered was protecting Tina. And hopefully getting them both out of this confrontation alive.

"I beg your pardon, miss, but do you happen to have any wine on the menu? I am greatly in need," the newcomer asked politely, though Zak could see that every word cost him.

Then he remembered what he'd heard about vampires and wine. The creature was seeking something that would help him, not attacking. That was a good sign. Zak keyed the mic, calling for Brody in low, urgent tones. Then he palmed his cell phone, hitting the speed dial that would bring the Alpha on the run.

"I'm sorry, sir, we don't serve alcohol. Our liquor license hasn't come through yet," Tina answered politely, though Zak could hear the confusion in her tone. Bless her little human heart, she didn't recognize the danger standing in her doorway.

Zak didn't take his eyes off the vampire. "Tina, don't you have some wine upstairs? Go get it, honey. Bring as many bottles as you can down here on the double. Leave them at the bottom of the stairs and then go back and get more. Everything you have. And then stay the hell upstairs for me, will you?"

She opened her mouth to argue. He could just feel it. But the vampire stepped forward and left a trail of blood across her doorstep. She gasped as the man's fangs showed.

"Get the fuck upstairs now, honey. And whatever you do, do *not* invite this guy up there. Vampires are big on invitations. Do *not* issue one, okay?"

"I won't. But Zak…" She sounded worried now.

Zak couldn't tell if she was concerned about him, or the bleeding bloodletter. Either way, she was a sweetheart for her concern, but right about now, with a vamp on the edge like this one clearly was, such weakness could easily get her killed.

"Take your bear's advice, little one. I am not to be trusted at the moment. I have lost too much blood. The wine might help," the bloodletter said as he all but collapsed into one of the chairs at the front of the bakery. He leaned back, blood and seawater pooling beneath him as he sat.

Zak didn't take his eyes off the man,

but—thank the Goddess—he heard Tina leave. Her scent went upstairs and she closed the door behind herself. Zak almost sighed in relief, but he was too keyed up to relax even that much. Everything in him recognized the threat that now sat in front of him.

"I'm Zak Flambeau, the town deputy," Zak introduced himself to the bloodletter, hoping the man could keep his wits a little longer.

Zak knew that bloodletters could go mad when starved of blood, either by being unable to feed, or bleeding from serious wounds, like this one. The red eyes gave it away. They were just on the good side of sanity right now, but that could change in an instant.

"I am Hiram Abernathy, master of this region. I am headquartered in Seattle, but was enjoying a few nights on the ocean when my yacht was attacked and destroyed by...something." The red eyes looked confused and sort of haunted. "I seek your aid and will apply to your Alpha for safe harbor, though as you seem to understand, I am *in extremis*. I need blood, or I will run mad. I am trying my best to stay sane at the moment."

"If I give you my blood, will you leave the girl alone?" Zak asked. He'd do anything to keep Tina safe.

To read more, get your copy of
Night Shift *by Bianca D'Arc.*

ABOUT THE AUTHOR

Bianca D'Arc has run a laboratory, climbed the corporate ladder in the shark-infested streets of lower Manhattan, studied and taught martial arts, and earned the right to put a whole bunch of letters after her name, but she's always enjoyed writing more than any of her other pursuits. She grew up and still lives on Long Island, where she keeps busy with an extensive garden, several aquariums full of very demanding fish, and writing her favorite genres of paranormal, fantasy and sci-fi romance.

Bianca loves to hear from readers and can be reached through Twitter (@BiancaDArc), Facebook (BiancaDArcAuthor) or through the various links on her website.

WELCOME TO THE D'ARC SIDE…
WWW.BIANCADARC.COM

OTHER BOOKS
BY BIANCA D'ARC

Paranormal Romance

Brotherhood of Blood
One & Only
Rare Vintage
Phantom Desires
Sweeter Than Wine
Forever Valentine
Wolf Hills*
Wolf Quest

Tales of the Were
Lords of the Were
Inferno

Tales of the Were ~ The Others
Rocky
Slade

Tales of the Were ~ Redstone Clan
The Purrfect Stranger
Grif
Red
Magnus
Bobcat
Matt

Dragon Knights
(continued)
The Ice Dragon**
Prince of Spies***
Wings of Change
FireDrake
Dragon Storm
Keeper of the Flame
Hidden Dragons
Sea Dragon

Science Fiction Romance

StarLords
Hidden Talent
Talent For Trouble
Shy Talent

Jit'Suku Chronicles ~ Arcana
King of Swords
King of Cups
King of Clubs
King of Stars
End of the Line

Jit'Suku Chronicles ~ Sons of Amber
Angel in the Badlands

Futuristic Erotic Romance

Resonance Mates
Hara's Legacy**
Davin's Quest
Jaci's Experiment
Grady's Awakening
Harry's Sacrifice

* RT Book Reviews Awards Nominee
** EPPIE Award Winner
*** CAPA Award Winner

WWW.BIANCADARC.COM

91846450R00083

Made in the USA
Middletown, DE
03 October 2018